Secret Surrender

by

Priscilla West

Table of Contents

Chapter One

I woke up cradled by a pair of tan, muscular arms and sighed contentedly. This time I knew immediately where I was: Vincent's bedroom. He was playing big spoon to my little, and as I lay there reminiscing, the previous twelve hours played through my memory in a pleasant haze. Vincent had, on balance, been very supportive about the situation with my ex-boyfriend Marty. I hadn't wanted to talk to him about it so early in our dating—I hadn't even told Riley until yesterday—but after seeing how it worked out I felt much better.

Turning over, I took in his handsome face breathing slowly and smoothly. His distinctive masculine scent was becoming familiar, which was both comforting and a major turn on. He slept like a man without a care in the world, and yet I knew anybody running a business as large as his had plenty to worry about. I admired his ability to deal with stress.

Over his shoulder I read the bright green digits of his alarm clock: it was only six-thirty. My mind immediately went to dirty places; my sex drive had always been mediocre at best but now it was through the roof.

I ran my hand down his sculpted abs toward the impressive cock below and was pleasantly surprised to find him hard. He had morning wood. It was difficult to take credit for turning him on while he was still sleeping, but wrapping my hand around him even through the soft cotton of his boxer briefs still made me wet. I softly ran my fingers up and down his shaft, eager to pull him out of his underwear.

He stirred. "Feel something you like?" he grunted sleepily. His eyes were half open and he looked sexy as he wiped them and yawned like a lion.

"I was feeling jealous of whoever was turning you on while you slept," I said coyly.

"You shouldn't be. You've been the only woman in my dreams for a while now."

I giggled, unsure if his claim could possibly be true. He knew what to say to make me feel special, at least.

"Nothing like the real thing, though." He kissed me on the forehead and moved his arm under me, cupping both buttocks through my underwear. "I like the way you look first thing in the morning."

I was sure my hair was a total mess, and my makeup was probably all over the place, but I blushed at the compliment anyway. Vincent, with his wavy hair and manly stubble, was built to look amazing right out of bed. I was jealous of how effortless it was for him to look as enticing as he did.

Leaving his erection for a moment, I planted my hand on his hard stomach and scooted myself up to smooch him on the lips.

He kissed me back more passionately than I'd anticipated, his tongue probing against my mouth. I broke the kiss and started another, this time ready, and our tongues wrestled playfully. I could see myself waking up to this on a more frequent basis.

Smiling against his mouth, I reached down toward his waist and slipped my hand beneath the elastic band of his underwear to grip the throbbing head of his cock. He was so hard I shuddered, imagining how he would feel inside of me. My pussy ached in anticipation of the way it would stretch around him.

His grip on my butt tensed before he picked me up and turned me onto my back, never breaking our kiss. Only once I was down did he grab the hand holding his cock and pin it to the bed.

He leaned down and nibbled on my ear, his hot breath tickling me. "I have to get to work," he whispered.

My heart sank. I'd been looking forward to one more round of sex before I had to return to reality. "Okay," I said.

When I moved to sit up, he smiled and easily pinned my shoulders down to the bed with his free hand.

"I said *I* have to get to work. *You* stay put."

Before I could answer him, he moved lower until his face was between my legs. I half straightened in surprise, ready to tell him he didn't have to do that, but quickly threw my head back on the pillow. My fingers gripped the sheets as the sensation of his tongue fluttering around my pussy radiated through my body.

He looked up at me and grinned.

"You remember me telling you that you have a beautiful cunt last night, right? Because it's gorgeous and glistening for me right now."

I closed my eyes. "It wants you inside," I said, not wanting to see the expression on his face. Talking dirty still made me feel uncomfortable but it was rapidly becoming second nature.

His hands left my legs and I felt the bed bounce up. "Keep your eyes closed," he said. I heard footsteps, then the sound of a wrapper being torn. "You like the suspense of not being able to see, don't you?"

I nodded and waited for the bed to bounce again with his weight.

Instead, his strong hands grabbed my thighs and he pulled me across his smooth bed sheets until I was on the bed's edge, legs high and spread. Exposed. He entered me swiftly, throwing me off balance. I opened my eyes afraid I was going to fall. I found his face and was comforted to see him smiling and holding me steady.

"You should trust me more," he said, thrusting slowly but steadily. "I told you I have a million ways to make you feel good and better."

He kissed me then scooped me up. I threw my arms around his neck and my legs around his waist as he placed one knee on the bed and then the other, all the while inside me. The muscles in his shoulders and back bulged. It was amazing how strong he was.

Once he had lowered me back onto his soft sheets, he began to move in and out quickly, building an even rhythm. I relaxed, slipping into a trance, my mind free of everything but the sensation of his body against mine, his cock inside me pushing against the walls of my sex.

The heat in my core radiated out into a blanket of sensual pleasure.

"You're so snug," he said, pumping.

He continued to move in and out of me with a steady rhythm. My climax was coming fast and I felt my muscles contracting in anticipation. He moaned in response and began thrusting harder, causing me to move my hips against him. Sex with Vincent was like nothing I'd ever experienced. It was exhausting and yet I wanted more and more.

"You're close, aren't you?" he said. "Come for me, Kristen. Now."

He thrust to the hilt and the orgasm slammed into me. My muscles tightened to their limit before my core burst and pleasure wracked my entire body. The sensation was at once too much and not enough; I moaned and thrust my hips out toward him, wanting to take all of his impressive length. I clenched around him and his cock jerked, which made me squeeze harder.

When my quivering had finally wound down, he gave one more mighty thrust then closed his eyes. Convulsions seized his lithe body as he came, the condom filling with his hot seed. I watched his face, fascinated, hardly believing I could make him feel such a strong sensation. It was an unfamiliar power trip.

"Damn it," he growled, pulling out of me and tying off the condom. He threw it in the trash and plopped down on his back, scooping me up after a second to my new favorite spot on his chest. "How am I ever going to get you off my mind when we have sex like that?"

"And why would I want to be off your mind?" I said coyly.

He gave me a small smile. Then his eyes glazed over as if he were looking off to the horizon. The subtle change in his demeanor was jarring. This must be another one of his sudden shifts. I didn't want to leave the bed and end the moment, much as I knew I had to, but I could tell for him the moment was already gone.

"Busy day?" I asked, raking my fingers up and down his chest.

Unmoving, he said nothing.

After a moment, I tried again. "Vincent, where are you?"

He shook his head as if warding off an unpleasant thought and looked down at me. His face was another derivative of charming Vincent. The man I'd been with earlier was gone.

"Sorry," he said. "Lots of work to do. Coffee?"

I hated that he could do that. How could he go from having passionate sex to being all business so quickly? Maybe it was something you had to put up with when you got involved with a man who ran a global empire, but it still bugged me. I nodded because I didn't trust myself to speak.

When I walked into his kitchen I was greeted by the sight of Vincent making an omelet in his light blue underwear.

His impressive bulge strained against the pima cotton even when he wasn't hard, and it left little to the imagination. With the way the morning light was pouring in his window, the scene looked like something out of a magazine ad—selling anything, so long as it included him.

It was a great recovery. "I didn't realize breakfast was being served with coffee," I said.

"Three egg omelet with red and green peppers, onion, jack cheese and ham. I hope that's all right. I'm a big believer in putting good things into your life if you want good things to come of it."

"Wise words." I wondered if Vincent thought of me as a good thing. Or if I thought of him as a good thing. We hadn't known each other very long; we were still getting to know one another. A good thing could easily turn into a bad one as I've figured out from experience. People can be surprising.

He winked. "And yes, you count as a good thing."

He flipped my omelet deftly onto a plate already containing sliced melon and strawberries and set it on the counter. Pouring me a fresh cup of coffee from a french press, he continued. "I have to go to Rio tonight. I'll be gone the rest of the week, but we need to keep in contact every day, especially since your ex found out where you live. Are you sure I can't put you up in a hotel or get you a guard?"

I took the coffee mug from his hand and took a sip, savoring the complex notes. It was so much better than the coffee at the office. "No," I said. "None of that will be necessary."

He nodded. "Okay, but after work we're going to the store before I leave and getting you some protection. Mace, at least. Something else as well. Maybe a gun."

I was touched he was so concerned about Marty, but I thought he was overreacting. We weren't dealing with a serial killer here. "That's fine, but I really think mace will be enough. I don't need an assault rifle or anything."

"Eat up, we do need to get to work soon," he said. "Want me to drop you off at a nearby subway station or at your building? I mean, you know, discretion and all."

"My building's fine," I said. The drop off would be quick enough and Vincent had tinted windows. It wouldn't be an issue to hide him taking me to work from my firm.

He shrugged. "Great. Remember, we need to hit the store after work, so no staying late."

I nodded. This swerve between business and affection was going to take some getting used to, but I could probably manage.

***

After getting dropped off in the high style of Vincent's old Camry, I walked into the office for my first day as a Client Acquisition Manager. Moving my things from my cubicle to my new office took up the first half of the morning. The office was going to be pretty sparse for a while, but it was mine. I was excited.

I planned on starting on some work on Vincent's account before lunch. I looked for the manila folder containing Vincent's signed contract along with other information about his assets but couldn't find it. I realized I must have left it with Richard. I'd have to get it from him.

My office was toward the end of the hall, which meant I had to walk almost the length of the floor to get to Richard's office. When I got there, I knocked and saw he was on the phone. He glanced at me briefly before gluing his eyes back to the screen.

I waited.

He was on the phone for almost ten minutes before he ended his conversation and got off. Still not glancing at me, he finally spoke. "Yes?"

I took a deep breath. "I think I left the Sorenson files with you. Can I have them?"

He continued typing. "You know those are with records by now."

"Okay, but I also know you made copies. Can I have those?"

He looked around before finally gracing me with a glance. "Listen, I'm very busy. Go down to records and have copies made there."

So this was how it was going to be. I understood his annoyance, but he was being a jerk about this. I knew he had to have copies of the file in his office somewhere. He would've had them made immediately, and he was so organized it would take him seconds to locate them.

"Richard—"

"I'm busy. Go down to records to get your files."

"I know you have them here somewhere. I'm happy to—"

"Is there anything else? For the hundredth time, I am very, very busy today."

I took a deep breath to calm myself. "No, that's all."

The right thing to do was let him be angry and not feed into it. Still, it hurt that he was being so rude to me. Maybe he was trying to keep me down even though we had the same title. Regardless, I'd have to put up with it for as long as I could.

I went down to records and wrestled with them to get the documents I needed. When I got back to my desk I found I'd received an email from my new boss, Carl Stansworth, asking me to drop by when I had a moment. "When I had a moment" really meant I needed to get there ASAP because he had a small opening in his schedule and wanted to see me during that time. I checked the timestamp and saw it had been sent eighteen minutes ago. That meant I didn't have long; guys like Carl booked themselves pretty full. I gathered up my stuff and rushed out of my office.

On the way to Carl's office—which occupied a corner on the opposite side of the floor from mine—I checked my phone and saw I had a text message from Vincent.

Hope your morning has been going well. Mine's been going steadily downhill.

Thoughts raced through my mind. What could have happened? I texted back asking what was wrong.

My phone buzzed again.

I'm not in bed with you right now, mostly.

Blushing furiously, I tapped out a quick reply.

This is a work phone! We have to be more discreet than that!

I shoved the device in my jacket pocket as I came to Carl's office. The door was closed. My phone buzzed as I looked around for his secretary. Spotting her, I walked over. "Carl asked me to drop by a minute ago. Do you know when he'll be free?"

As I waited for her to finish typing, I glanced down at my phone to read Vincent's message.

Fine. Your performance managing my assets this morning was exemplary. I have ideas for some new positions we could take that I want to share at our next meeting.

"—was your name, honey?" I snapped to attention, feeling the heat in my cheeks again as I worked to push Vincent's message from my mind. She must have been asking who I was so she could buzz Carl. I needed to focus at work or else my performance would suffer at the worst possible moment.

Before I could respond, I heard Carl's voice from behind me.

"Kristen, come on in." I turned to face him and he nodded at my phone. "Impossible to get away these days, right? I admire you young people for being so good at managing all these devices. I want to throw mine through the window once or twice a day." His green eyes twinkled behind gold framed glasses. The way his face wrinkled when he smiled combined with the white hair on the sides of his head—he was bald on top—showed his age, but he owned it and generally exuded an air of happiness.

I shoved it into my pocket and laughed politely. "That would be a pretty serious liability if it hit someone."

Carl chuckled as he led me into his office. "You could have been a lawyer if you weren't doing this. Maybe you should talk to them; they're the ones making me mad enough to throw the thing half the time."

I did my best fake smile. He sat down and motioned for me to take the seat across from him.

"So," he said, clasping his hands on the desk, "Vincent Sorenson. First of all, congratulations on landing that one. Tough prospect. Second, what's your plan to keep him?" He smiled and looked at me expectantly.

I wished I had been given more time to research what to do with Vincent's account before talking to Carl about it. Since I hadn't had enough time, I decided to stay vague. "Well, the bond market has some pretty promising sectors, so I'm thinking we can start there."

He nodded. "Sure. The thing is, a guy like that is going to want big returns. He's used to taking risks and reaping the rewards."

I bit my lip. He had a point. "True, which is why I also wanted to suggest a plan targeting BRIC assets. There's more risk there but those economies have been performing very well for a while and I think he'll be interested in the international flavor."

His eyes widened and he held out his fingers. "I think Brazil is the only one with surfing out of those, right? Russia definitely not, and I'm not sure about India but I know I'd only go surfing off the coast of China if I wanted to commit suicide by pollution." He laughed. All anyone at the firm seemed to know about Vincent was he was rich and enjoyed surfing.

"Do you surf?" I blurted.

He laughed even harder. "It was a hypothetical. Can you imagine me surfing?"

I shrugged and wracked my brain for a useful nugget from the research I had done on Vincent's company before the pitch. "Actually, India has lots of great surfing, and his company has been targeting China as a new growth market. Apparently there are people going out on the water there, though I imagine they're avoiding the river mouths."

Still chuckling, Carl nodded. "Shows what I know about that stuff. I like this BRIC plan. Focus on that, and present the safer bond strategy as a backup if you need it. We're going to get some analysts working under you, but that will take a while because people are wrapping up other jobs, so for now you're going to be on your own. Knowing your work ethic, I'm sure you won't mind the longer hours in the interim."

I nodded, eager to get back to my desk and see if this plan was even remotely viable. This is what happened when you weren't prepared: you had to make stuff up and it might not work out.

"Anything else for me?" he asked.

I shook my head. "No. I do think Vincent will like this BRIC plan. He's actually flying to Rio tonight for a product launch."

He furrowed his brow. "How do you know that?"

Great question—how did I know that? Beyond the truth, of course. This whole seeing a client thing was going to keep me on my toes.

"I saw a news story about it," I said, scrambling. "I have Google Alerts set up for his name and his company. Just saw the story before I walked over here actually." It didn't explain why I knew he was flying over tonight, but hopefully it would be enough of an answer for him not to push me on it.

It was. He shook his head. "It's been so long since I was an analyst, I feel out of the loop. Great to see young blood getting their feet wet. I'm predicting great things from this account, Kristen." He stood up and I did the same before he motioned me to the door. "I have a lunch meeting now, but keep me posted on how things are going and let me know if you need anything."

With another nod, I left.

I was taking deep breaths to stop myself from hyperventilating all the way back to my office. When I got there, I closed the door behind me and sat in the dark. Meeting with Carl would have been stressful in itself, but adding in the situation with Vincent made it even more so. Thankfully, it seemed to have gone well. Carl liked me, which was more important than Richard liking me, since Carl was my new boss.

I knew better than to go to Carl about anything Richard was doing unless it was absolutely necessary. Bosses were a lot like clients: they wanted you to make their lives easier and make them money. Giving Carl a situation to deal with was the best way to make sure he liked me less.

Other than losing him money. That would be worse.

I got up and flicked the light on in my office before checking my phone. No new messages. I tapped out a belated reply to Vincent's earlier message about taking up new positions at our next meeting.

Probably not our next meeting, right? I don't think they will let us fool around at the store.

Seconds later, I got a reply.

Oh right, I meant in my daydreams about you. Make sure you get out of work as close to 5 as possible. It might be a little tight to catch my charter down there.

I suddenly felt bad. He was so busy and I was burdening him. Even though he was still doing his best to squeeze me in his schedule, I was definitely making his life more hectic. This shopping trip was probably going to work out, but I almost wished I had kept my mouth shut about Marty. It was hard to argue this wasn't a negative element in whatever was going on between us.

I sat staring at my phone, thinking of what to text back, but there was nothing to really say. The best I could do was apologize when he arrived, because he wasn't going to take no for an answer at this point. Once he set his mind on something, he followed through. Getting me protection items was evidence of that.

The rest of the day passed in a swirl of research and note taking. It looked like the BRIC strategy would be doable, to my relief. I could start preparing materials for my next business meeting with Vincent soon.

First though, there would be another non-business meeting.

At 4:59, I packed up my stuff and left the office earlier than I had in months. I knew Vincent would be waiting for me in his Camry by the time I got down.

***

"I thought we were going to the grocery store to get mace," I said as I stared at a sign with a rifle and knife crossed over one another like crossbones. Bold letters read 'Army and Navy Surplus'. The towering brick facade was almost as intimidating as what I imagined they sold inside. Vincent had driven us to the outskirts of the city on the pretense that there was an awesome grocery store there with lots of free food samples. But as I looked at the barren strip of highway to my right and the stretch of farmland to my left I knew we were miles from any grocery store.

"I knew you would've protested to coming out here, but I wasn't going to take no for an answer. You need to protect yourself, Kristen."

He was right, I would have protested—we hadn't even gone inside yet and I was already itching to leave. Having weapons lying around my apartment was only going to make me more nervous about Marty making a reappearance. If I admitted to myself that I needed protection then I was also admitting that he was a legitimate threat to my safety, and I didn't want to revisit that thought.

"Martin probably realized it was a bad idea to stop by my apartment," I began, trying to convince him that the trip was unnecessary. "I bet he's already gone." I knew Vincent felt strongly about my safety but I was determined not to be treated like some damsel in distress.

He turned to me, his lips set into a thin line. "This is about more than that. You're a young woman living in the city . . . I need to be sure that no one can hurt you."

"Vincent, you can't save me from everything."

"I can try."

I nearly blushed at his sincerity. Maybe I wasn't ready to face the severity of the situation I was in, but Vincent was—I'd never seen him so persistent, and he certainly didn't have anything to gain from bringing me here. My earlier fears that my relationship history had lessened his feelings for me were quickly dissipating.

Still, I tried to imagine what we would find in Army and Navy Surplus that would be of any use to me and came up empty—I envisioned gun-lined walls and cases of sharpened knives. I'd never so much as used a sling shot, let alone a real weapon.

"Well, you should know that I've never fired a gun or anything before," I admitted bashfully.

Vincent took me by the hand. "Let's look around first. We'll find you something you're comfortable with."

I rolled my eyes as he ushered me through the entrance to the store, but I wasn't going to argue with him since we were already here.

The inside resembled a massive warehouse and I was immediately hit by the sight of military accessories— army jackets, yucca packs, deactivated hand grenades, and antique first aid kits were only a few of the items that decorated the storefront. Beyond us lay conveniently labeled aisles for "cooking," "outdoors," and "defense." I swallowed a hard lump as I considered the last one.

"Some of this is just for show," Vincent said, gesturing to a set of novelty dog tags. "The stuff we're looking for is locked in display cases near the back."

As I fingered the length of an empty bullet casing poised on a nearby shelf I wondered why Vincent knew so much about this place, down to its very layout.

"Have you been here before?"

"Just a few times. When I was living from place to place after college I needed supplies I could rely on, things that wouldn't break down. I got so used to shopping at places like this that I guess I never broke the habit."

It was hard to imagine Vincent roughing it after having seen his house, but I knew he hadn't always lived a privileged lifestyle.

"I also learned that you need to be able to defend yourself," he added.

"What did you need to defend yourself against?"

"Nothing serious. People would sometimes try to take advantage of us, steal from us, because we were young and seemed vulnerable. It's funny, even when you become successful you find yourself dealing with the same thing."

"I guess I was young and vulnerable, too," I admitted, thinking of how clueless I was when I began dating Marty. "Just in a different way."

"Now you won't be." He put his hand on the small of my back and urged me forward. We made our way toward the defense section, bypassing a few shoppers, but the place was nearly empty.

As we approached the back of the store I spotted a glass display case that stretched at least ten feet across. Its shelves were illuminated from below so that the items crowded onto them seemed to glow.

A middle-aged man came out from a door behind the case, cleaning the barrel of shotgun with a rag. He had thinning grey hair cropped short to his head. He wore a forest-green jacket overloaded with pockets. A gray shirt underneath covered a paunch belly draping slightly over a pair of army cargo pants. His arms were so muscled that he seemed to be walking with his chest permanently puffed out.

"Can I help you?" he asked in a distinctive accent as we approached him. The name tag pinned to his t-shirt read "Darryl."

"We're just looking for some protective equipment," Vincent answered.

"This is the place for it. What kind of protection are we talking about?"

I wondered how many different things you could defend yourself from, but the length of the display case suggested there were plenty.

"Something she can use if she finds herself in . . . a bind." His mouth twisted. Vincent was taking the threat of Marty very seriously.

Darryl's eyes widened. "A bind, huh? I've got just the thing. Give me a minute." He disappeared behind the door he came out of earlier, leaving Vincent and me alone.

"Maybe I should just leave town with you," I teased as I turned to him, leaning my hip into the display case. "He can't find me if I'm not here, right?"

Vincent seemed to stiffen at the mention of his trip but quickly reached up to cup my chin in his hand, gently running the pad of his thumb across my jaw line. "You can't put your life on hold because of this, Kristen."

"I know," I sighed, leaning into his touch. "A vacation just sounds nice right now."

"The trip is going to be anything but vacation."

"What are you doing in Rio?" I asked as I realized that he hadn't told me much about the details of his trip.

"We're throwing a launch party for a new product," he said, dropping his hand from my face.

"What kind of product?"

"We're releasing a new surfboard in South America and there's a big party to publicize it. There's going to be famous stars, business people, media—the usual."

Thoughts flooded my head of the women surrounding him at the bar in Cape Town. I'd wondered why he hadn't told me about the party earlier, but I tried to chalk it up to distraction. After all, I had given him a lot to think about. "Sounds like vacation to me."

"In this business even parties are work."

I was just about to ask him for more details about what kind of people would be there, worried that a launch party in Brazil would be as wild as it sounded, when Darryl reemerged. He had a silver revolver in his hand that looked like he reached into a television and pulled it out of a Dirty Harry movie.

"This is a Ruger SP101. It'll take some getting used to especially with your small hands. I'd take it out to the firing range a few times to get a handle on it and build up some callouses."

I shot Vincent a doubtful look but he gestured for me to try it. *Really?*

Darryl placed the gun in my outstretched palm and I had to use my other hand to help support the weight.

"How does it feel?" Vincent asked.

Like I'm holding a bowling ball.

"I'm not sure this is going to work," I replied.

Darryl wrinkled his brows and scratched his chin. "Okay, I got something better." He went into the back room again and reappeared. This time he was carrying a large, steel tube with a trigger attached to its bottom.

"This is an M1 rocket launcher," Darryl said, his voice raising an octave with excitement. "It'll obliterate any 'binds' you might find yourself in. Try it out, see how it feels."

Darryl thrust the rocket launcher into my hands before I had a chance to protest. I stood, awkwardly bearing the heavy weight, unsure how I was even supposed to hold it. I unwittingly laughed from the overkill.

"I'm not sure I can fit this in my purse," I joked.

"How about something a little more discreet?" Vincent asked, taking the rocket launcher from my hands and setting it on the display case.

"Well, we've got these over here." Darryl scurried over to the end of the case, beckoning us to follow him with a frantic wave of the hand. He pulled a knife from its shelf and unsheathed it, revealing its thick and serrated edge.

"This"—a wide and crooked smile spread across his face—"is an OKC-3S Bayonet. This is a real bang for your buck, multi-purpose, you know, not just for defense. But if that's what you're looking for, a defense weapon, this will get them every time." He thrust the handle of the knife at me, his own fingers digging into the blade.

"Try it," he insisted.

"I think I'll just . . . look."

He shrugged, as if to say suit yourself. "If you're looking for discreet, this is it." He stuck the knife back into its sheath and slipped it into the hip pocket of his cargo pants. "Can't even see it."

"Don't you think this is all a little overkill?" I asked to both men. They both looked at me, surprised.

"You can never be too prepared, honey," Darryl said.

Vincent nodded.

Ugh. Men.

I exhaled heavily, which seemed to make Vincent come to his senses.

"It's a beautiful knife," Vincent said, his charming business persona taking over. "But I think we're more interested in something like this." He pointed to a row of silver necklaces spread across the top shelf of the case, a different pendant attached to each chain. The quaint pieces of jewelry looked out of place next to the weapons that surrounded them.

"Ah, these are very popular," Darryl said as he set the knife down next to the rocket launcher, much to my relief.

"A necklace?" I asked, turning to Vincent.

"Not quite."

"Which one are you interested in?" Darryl asked.

Vincent looked at me contemplatively, as if considering which pendant would suit me best, before turning back to the case. "That one."

Darryl pulled one of the necklaces from the bunch and held it up, a small heart-shaped locket spinning from the chain. He showed me the bottom of the heart which contained a small hole.

"You can insert a mace cartridge into the back," Vincent said, taking the necklace from Darryl and laying the heart flat on his palm. He flipped it open to reveal a small canister, its nozzle situated into the hole.

"You just squeeze the heart in the center to shoot the mace." He draped the necklace around my neck and fastened it.

I looked down at it, afraid to even touch it for fear of setting it off inside. "I don't know, Vincent. What if someone knocks into me and it goes off?"

"There's a safety switch," Darryl cut in. "See the small button on the side? You have to slide it down to be able to use it. If you're in trouble you won't have to reach into your purse, these necklaces are one of our best sellers because they're so convenient."

"Kristen, if someone attacks you, you'll be able to defend yourself without inflicting any real damage to them. All I want is to be able to protect you, and this is the only way I know how. I can't always be there." He reached out and touched the pendant, his fingers brushing against my exposed clavicle. The gesture was tender and so were his words. If it would make Vincent feel better knowing that I could defend myself then I didn't see the harm in wearing the necklace. In fact, the idea of having something so accessible already felt like a small comfort to me.

"All right, I'll take it," I said.

"We'll get one for Riley too," Vincent said.

"Riley already has her own."

"But is it a necklace? It'll be more convenient than whatever she's carrying around in her purse."

It was a good suggestion. Although Marty had been cordial with Riley the first time he stopped by, I knew his mood could escalate, and quickly. I didn't want her to be collateral damage.

I nodded in agreement.

"I also think you should have something else, just in case the mace isn't enough," he added.

"I've got just the thing," Darryl said, reaching below the display case. I imagined him pulling out a flamethrower or a chainsaw so I was almost taken aback by the simplicity of the small rectangular device he set in front of us. "It's a taser. If the mace doesn't subdue him, this will. Guaranteed."

I picked it up and pressed its button, jumping as a bright blue electric current ignited at the taser's end.

"This seems dangerous."

"It will hurt someone, no doubt. But not permanently," Darryl assured me.

"It'll be a last resort item," Vincent said. "Just keep it in your purse."

I could think of a million ways something could go wrong with the necklace—I could forget to wear it one day, it could break, or get ripped from my neck. Having a backup plan couldn't hurt.

"Better safe than sorry," I conceded.

Vincent smiled and pushed the taser and necklace toward Darryl. "And a few extra mace cartridges," he said. "So she can practice."

I turned to Vincent as Darryl rang us up. "Well, if Marty does show up he'll be sorry," I tried to laugh off my unease.

"He can't hurt you now, Kristen. I won't let it happen." He reached out and brushed the hair from my face, and I found myself wishing he didn't have to leave town—the mace and the taser were helpful, but neither of them could make me feel as safe as Vincent did.

Vincent paid for the items, by his insistence of course, but at least this time they were cheaper than a day of surfing. As we left the store and approached his car he put his arm around my shoulder and pulled me into him. "You know, I think that rocket launcher suited you."

"I could barely hold it!"

He leaned me against the driver's side door; his hands settled into the groove of my waist. "You've handled more powerful things."

"Powerful, yes," I teased, rising up onto the tips of my toes to bring my mouth close to his. "But not as big."

His hold on my waist tightened as he gripped at the fabric of my shirt, balling it up in his fists as if he wanted to tear it from me.

"I've never heard you complain." He planted a hard kiss onto my lips and I almost dropped my shopping bag, the sensation of his skin against mine sending a wave of desire through me. Worried that other shoppers might catch us in our heated embrace, I broke away from the kiss.

"Too bad it's not big enough to reach from Brazil to New York City," I said.

"What's your schedule like tomorrow?" he asked as we got into the car.

"I'll be pretty tied up all day. I have a meeting with Carl and then I need to review some things on your account. Why?"

"Just because I'll be in South America doesn't mean I don't want to see you, what about video chat tomorrow night? How's seven?"

I leaned close to him, breathing in the sharp scent of his cologne. "It's a date."

Chapter Two

Vincent swung by a Duane Reade so I could grab Riley a few more cold remedies and then dropped me off at my apartment. I hated to say goodbye so suddenly but I knew he needed to get to the airport to catch his flight.

I climbed the flight of stairs in my apartment building to my floor and saw two guys carrying boxes into the apartment across from me. One was tall and leanly muscular with a striped shirt stretching against his torso that seemed two sizes too small for his build. The other was short and stout with broad shoulders and bulging biceps. The odd duo reminded me of Mario and Luigi.

A cd fell out of the box the short guy was carrying and I stooped to pick it up.

"Here, you dropped this." As I held out the cd, I looked at the cover. There was some weird picture of a sphinx— head of a man, body of a lion—except the head was female and the body was a motorcycle. The title read "Born This Way by Lady Gaga".

He set the box he was carrying on the floor inside, smiled, and took the cd from me. "Thank you so much. Can't imagine going for long without these catchy tunes." His smile widened and he offered his large hand. "Bernie."

I shook it. "Kristen."

He gestured to his tall friend who was unpacking kitchen items. "And that's Kurt."

"Hello." I waved. "Welcome to the building."

Kurt smiled and waved back. "Are you in the unit just across from us?"

"Yep, the one with the blue 'home sweet home' doormat in front."

"Great to meet the neighbors!" He grinned.

After exchanging pleasantries, Kurt and Bernie returned to their business, but not before inviting Riley and I over for dinner sometime after they'd finished settling in. They seemed like a nice couple.

I opened my front door to find Riley curled up in a blanket on the couch, a steaming mug cupped in her hands. At least she was sitting up, a noticeable improvement from the last few days.

"Vick's vapor rub, moisturized tissues, and cough drops—strawberry flavored, of course." I set the bag of items on the dining room table along with my bag of protective gear and flopped onto the couch beside her.

"You're the best," Riley said, her voice still nasally. "But I still wouldn't sit too close, I don't want to get you sick. Vincent would probably never forgive me if a cold kept you from seeing him."

"Actually, he's leaving for Brazil tonight for a launch party." I tried to keep my voice even, not wanting to betray the jealousy that was lingering faintly in the back of my mind.

"So that means I can cough in your general direction?" she joked.

"No," I rolled my eyes. "But it does mean I'm staying in. And I need your help with something if you're feeling up to it."

"Okay. What's going on?"

I wrung my hands nervously, knowing that if I told Riley about the mace and taser I'd have to tell her about Marty, too. But she deserved to hear the truth, especially if there was a chance that she'd have to deal with him again. "I remember you had mace when we were in Cape Town and Vincent just bought me some. I was wondering if you could show me how to use it?"

"Mace?" she asked as she set her mug down and turned to me. "Is this about your ex?"

"Yes. I haven't heard from him since the day he stopped by, but I just wanted to be prepared."

"Prepared for what, Kristen? You still haven't told me what happened with him."

I hesitated, but the idea of finally revealing my past to Riley brought with it a sense of relief. "I met Marty in a business finance class," I began. "I was a Junior and he was a Senior. We flirted a little but it wasn't until he was my TA the following year that we really hit it off."

"Your TA, huh?" she teased. "Ms. Harvard Grad sleeping with the teacher, I almost don't believe it."

I shot her a wry side glance, but I had to admit that Riley knew how to make a difficult situation bearable.

"He was only a year older than me," I said. "Not to mention gorgeous, smart, and completely charming. All of the girls in my class had a crush on him." My stomach churned at the thought of Marty at the beginning of our relationship—the romantic dates, the small but sweet gestures, the intimate conversations. That version of him seemed so distant from the guy he turned into.

"So why exactly are you afraid of him? You practically fled the apartment the other night."

"Things were great between us for the first few months. He seemed like a catch. But when the pressures of post-college life started getting to him he became jealous and possessive." I swallowed a hard lump as I recalled the scathing names he called me, the minor but frightening ways he would grab me when I challenged him.

"I know that's not healthy," Riley said, cocking her eyebrow. "But it doesn't exactly make him dangerous. What aren't you telling me?"

I sighed and looked Riley in the eye, preparing to admit to her what I'd been hiding for so long. "Marty has borderline personality disorder, but I didn't discover that until a year into our relationship. He could turn from charming to vicious in a matter of seconds. He would call me names if he thought I was flirting with another guy, sometimes he'd get aggressive—"

Riley threw the blanket from her shoulders, seemingly agitated. "Aggressive? Are you saying he hit you, Kristen?"

"No, he never hit me. But . . ." I held up my crooked pinky finger.

She reached for my hand frantically and squeezed it gently with her own. "Oh my god, Kristen. Why didn't you tell someone?"

"He comes from a powerful family. I couldn't tell anyone about it. Not even the police. So I left . . . changed my address, found a new job, and hoped he'd move on. But somehow he's found me, and I'm not sure what he wants."

"Well now I feel like a complete jerk for pushing you to date, I had no idea you were dealing with this."

I smiled at Riley's concern, feeling I had made the right decision by telling her. "How could you have known?"

She looked up at me and twisted her mouth as if she had something she wanted to say but was afraid to say it.

"You can ask me anything, Riley. It's fine."

"How did you deal with it? It must have been scary . . . being with someone who could turn on you at any second."

Silence settled over us as I considered her question. Had I dealt with it? I'd been pretty much avoiding the thought of Marty since I left Boston and even now, with the possibility of him in my city, I was still trying to push the memory of my relationship with him from my mind.

"For a long time I tried to act like it wasn't a big deal, like maybe it was a phase. But after the pinky incident I left as fast as I could and I guess I haven't really dealt with it, not until now."

"Have you told Vincent?"

"Yeah, and then he hauled me out to the middle of nowhere to buy me mace and a taser."

"A taser?" Her eyebrows shot up. "You'll definitely have to show me that."

"Don't you think it's overkill?"

A seriousness settled over Riley's face as she scooted closer to me. "This guy could come back, Vincent just wants you to be safe. And so do I."

"Then maybe he shouldn't have jetted off to Brazil." I felt my cheeks grow hot with embarrassment as I realized how childish I sounded.

"Isn't he just going for business?"

"Cape Town was business, too, but you saw him at the bar . . . women flock to him." I tried not to picture bikini clad models latching onto Vincent's arm and feeding him drinks all night.

"But Vincent doesn't flock to other women. Kristen, the guy bought you a taser."

I laughed as my hand instinctively wandered to the necklace he'd put on me earlier that day. Riley was right. I'd never seen Vincent so attentive or concerned as he was when we were at the army surplus store—it felt good to be with someone who cared about my safety instead of threatening it.

"Will you show me how to use this?" I said, eyeing the necklace between my fingers.

"That's the mace?"

"He got you one, too." I walked over to the dining room table and pulled the extra mace cartridges from the bag as well as the necklace we had picked out for Riley, a star shaped pendant dangling from the end.

"This is definitely more convenient than that bulky brick I've been carrying around in my purse!" she said as I handed her the necklace.

We left the living room and stepped out onto the balcony so we wouldn't chance inhaling the spray. After Riley showed me how to insert the cartridge and where to press in order to set it off, we practiced shooting mace at a potted plant. After a dozen or so attempts, we both felt confident in our accuracy and quickdraw. We also felt sorry for the plant.

Although the practice was a much needed tension reliever, I couldn't believe I was in this position again, only this time I was actually preparing for Marty's possible attack instead of ignoring it.

"Are you okay?" Riley asked, seemingly sensing my unease.

"I just can't believe this is happening." I looked out over the balcony at the glinting lights of the city in the distance, wondering if Marty was still out there.

"We're doing this to make sure he doesn't hurt you again." She put her hand on my shoulder and I nodded, acknowledging her concern. "But we probably shouldn't test out the taser." She laughed.

I smirked. "We wouldn't want you couch-ridden again."

"Speaking of couch-ridden, I should probably rest."

"Me, too," I said as I realized how exhausted I was. "It's been the longest day."

We went inside and each disappeared into our rooms. I took off the necklace and placed it on my bedside table, still nervous that I might accidentally set it off in my sleep, and hid the taser in my closet. I would tackle that one another day.

As I climbed into bed, I found myself thinking of Vincent's trip to Brazil and realized that I no longer felt so nervous about it. I couldn't deny that he was attractive and that other women would always respond to that. But for the first time since Marty showed up I didn't feel so scared. In fact, I felt in control.

Chapter Three

I tried not to let my nerves get the best of me when I got to work the next day. I wasn't sure what my meeting with Carl was for, only that he wanted me in his office at noon. The morning went slowly, my anticipation of the meeting causing me to look at the clock every few minutes. The dragging time made it hard to push thoughts of Vincent's business trip from my mind. I hadn't heard from him since he left. I knew he was busy but he could've at least managed a text.

Although I had Vincent to thank for the greater sense of security I now felt with my mace and taser on hand, I couldn't shake the lingering sense of jealousy I felt every time I thought of the launch party. Bikini clad models would no doubt be there to show off the new surfboard, and there would certainly be no shortage of alcohol. Vincent said it himself—he wasn't used to taking things slow, and he definitely wasn't used to commitment, how could I compete with models when I was on an entirely different continent?

I tried to distract myself with work—skimming the accounts of a few potential clients and answering emails throughout the morning. When it was finally noon I made my way to Carl's office, stopping in the bathroom to make sure I looked presentable, before giving a light knock on the door. A low voice called from behind it, telling me to come in.

I opened the door and stepped into his office. It was almost as impressive as Vincent's—a view of the Hudson River Park served as a stunning backdrop for plush leather office chairs, a glossy hardwood desk, and chrome fixtures that gave the space a classic but contemporary touch. Carl was poised over an open file, a silver pen flicking quickly across the pages inside.

"Good afternoon Mr. Stansworth."

Carl immediately looked up from his work and gave me a smile, a refreshing change from Richard, who could barely tear his eyes from his phone. His remaining gray hairs were neatly combed. Although he had crow's feet beneath his eyes, he was sprightly and kept in good health. "Afternoon Kristen, why don't you take a seat?"

I sank into the black cushioned chair across from his desk, the nervous energy I had worked up earlier hitting me full force as I contemplated why Carl had called the meeting. Had Richard complained about my performance? Did Carl know about me and Vincent? I'd never forgive myself if I'd let an attraction ruin my career.

"You're probably wondering why I've asked you into my office this afternoon," he said as he carefully capped his pen and set it aside, focusing his attention on me.

I swallowed and tried not to betray my panic as I answered him. "Yes, sir."

"Well, I'd like to start off by saying that you've done good work on the Sorenson account." A warm smile spread across his face as he spoke. I breathed a sigh of relief as I realized that I wasn't going to be demoted or, worse, fired for dating a client. "We knew he would be difficult to land, but you did it."

The nervous energy I had been feeling earlier began to dissipate with Carl's encouraging words. It felt good to be recognized for the work I'd done, especially without the assumptions that my "feminine allure" had anything to do with it. Still, Richard was integral in researching Vincent and formulating our strategy for our first presentation—I really couldn't have done it without his help. "Thank you," I said. "But Richard did a lot of work on that account, too. I can't take all the credit."

"Richard played his part, but you closed the deal. That's what matters on an account like this, so congratulations. You earned that promotion."

"Thank you Mr. Stansworth."

"And that's why I've asked you in here today, I was hoping you could give me your opinion on a prospect we've been trying to land for a few weeks now."

I hoped I wasn't blushing, but I was flattered that Carl trusted me enough to consult me on a pitch I wasn't even assigned to. "Who's the client?"

"Michael Cohen, are you familiar?"

Anyone who worked at Waterbridge-Howser would recognize the name; in fact, most of the firms in New York City had been trying to take him on as a client ever since he dropped Ellis-Kravitz as his wealth management firm two months prior. "Of course," I said. "He owns the most profitable industrial machinery company on the East Coast and is looking to expand cross country. I thought he had already decided to go with Waterbridge-Howser?"

"So did I, but we recently found out that he took a meeting with Watson-James. We're scheduled for a follow up pitch tomorrow but I think we need to rework our strategy—clearly it didn't work the first time."

I hadn't reviewed the materials, and I was worried that I wouldn't be able to suggest anything useful. "I'm not sure I can be of much help," I admitted.

He opened a desk drawer below him and rummaged around for a minute before producing a thick manila folder. "I wouldn't have asked for your help if I didn't think you were capable, Kristen. Just take a look at this file," he said as he handed the folder to me. "These are the documents from our initial meeting with Cohen. I'd like to hear any ideas you might have on a new approach."

I browsed the contents of the folder, comparing the initial proposal to the limited knowledge I had of Cohen's company. Feeling emboldened by Carl's confidence in me, I decided to point out the first inconsistency that I saw, hoping not to step on any feet. I took a deep breath, formulated my thoughts, and spoke. "The initial approach was strong, the emphasis on his expansion is key. But I think you might benefit from a broader focus on the strongholds he already has on the East Coast. Especially with the risk he's taking by expanding, we need to reassure him of the solid platform we can build using his current assets. I think we need to show him that we're invested in the business he's already built, not just his potential for the future."

Carl twisted his mouth in apparent consideration, and I began to worry I'd insulted him. I wasn't used to being consulted on large accounts; Richard was more of a delegator, leaving me to deal with prep work like charts and graphs rather than formulating strategy.

"Where do you think we can best incorporate that information into the follow-up pitch we already have?" Carl asked.

"In my opinion," I began, clearing my throat nervously, "it should be the first thing you emphasize. It will show him that you respect his company and also make for a smoother transition into the points on expansion."

He shook his head slowly. "Watson-James is known for tradition. Cohen probably met with them when he realized our approach was future focused. Great catch, Kristen. You may have saved yet another account, keep it up."

I tried to hold back the beaming smile that was threatening to creep across my face as I handed the folder back to him. "Thank you Mr. Stansworth, let me know if there's anything else I can do for you."

I left Carl's office feeling more confident in my job than I ever had while working for Richard. Instead of treating me like his inferior or some prop, Carl treated me like his peer. I had to admit that I'd learned a lot from Richard—mostly by figuring things out on my own—but I had a feeling that working with Carl would be far more hands on. I couldn't help but think that, although I'd earned my new position at Waterbridge-Howser through hard work, my new career success wouldn't have been possible had I never met Vincent.

As I approached my desk I felt my phone vibrating in my pocket. I pulled it out to look at it and my stomach did a flip when I saw who it was from: Vincent. We'd been seeing each other for a few weeks now, but I still found myself getting excited every time I heard from him.

All work . . . I'm ready for some play, still on for Skype at 7 your time?

I was relieved to know that he was thinking about me despite how busy he must have been with the launch party. My earlier jealousy was starting to seem irrational—if Vincent wanted casual sex he could have it. It certainly would have been easier than dating, but he was cutting time out of his schedule for me. He was adjusting.

I typed a response. *It's a date, but there might be a little work involved.*

Only for you. Talk later.

I smiled as I put my phone away. Vincent might have been a bad boy once, but it seemed that things were changing.

***

On my way home, I ran across Kurt, who was on his way to pick up take-out from a Chinese restaurant nearby. We exchanged a few pleasantries. I told him I worked for a wealth management firm and he told me he worked security. I wasn't sure what that meant exactly but it wasn't hard to imagine him being a bouncer with his height and muscles.

When I got inside the apartment, the air was hotter than normal. Riley was laying on the couch as usual but in her work clothes, her bag next to the coffee table. It looked like she plopped down as soon as she made it inside. Must've been a hard day at work.

"Yeesh, why is it so hot in here?" I asked.

"The air conditioning is busted and it's like ninety degrees outside. Thank goodness for global warming and summer, right?" Riley replied, eyes closed and back of her hand resting on her forehead.

"I feel like we should be getting a tan in this heat. Are they going to fix it?"

"Yeah, I called the landlord. He said other people complained and he has a guy already working on it."

"That's good news." I slipped out of my shoes and put on some slippers. Moving on, I asked, "Did you go to work today?"

"I was feeling well enough to go in around noon. But I'm definitely sleeping early tonight. My head's still congested."

"I'm glad to hear you're better."

"How was your day?" she asked.

"Nothing too exciting. I had a meeting with my new boss. Carl's much better than Richard—who by the way is starting to be a pain in the ass. He thinks I stole Vincent from him."

"I saw you hold a poisonous spider." Her hand leaped from her forehead to point at me. "You definitely deserved Vincent more than he did."

I shrugged. "He doesn't know that though. And I'd like to keep it that way." I dropped my bag beside the kitchen table.

"So, other than work." She straightened herself on the couch and brushed her strawberry-blonde hair behind her ears. Her blue eyes looked at me carefully. "How are you doing?" she asked delicately.

I leaned against a kitchen chair and shifted my feet. "I'm okay. It's been on my mind but I feel a lot better and safer since Monday. Vincent's been out of town but he's checking up on me regularly, which is nice."

"That's good to hear, Kristen. I'm really happy for you. It sounds like Vincent really cares about you."

He'd been unexpectedly supportive since I told him about Marty. Any other guy would've probably made an awkward excuse to avoid me and I wouldn't blame them. Most people were busy battling their own problems; they weren't going to fight somebody else's—no matter how good the sex.

"I think I really care about him."

She smiled. "As you should. How did things go at his place?"

I felt my cheeks blush. "It was good. He made dinner for us. I found out what an awesome chef he is."

"A great cook as well? God, I'm not even going to lie to you, Kristen. I'm so jealous."

I laughed. "Thanks, I guess."

"So." Her eyes turned wicked. "Did you get some action?"

I smiled bashfully and tried to look away from her curious eyes.

She beamed and pointed her finger at me again. "I knew it."

I recounted the rest of the night at Vincent's place to Riley, only leaving out the most intimate details—which were the ones she wanted to hear most. I could trust her not to tell anyone, but I didn't feel ready to have a detailed discussion about my newly invigorated sex life. I was still trying to wrap my head around it. After over two years without sex, I'd just had it three times with nipple-pierced bad boy Vincent Sorenson. Blindfolds and multiple orgasms? What *could* I make of that?

Besides being the best sex of my life.

Riley seemed satisfied with the rundown even without the graphic details. I knew she'd probably prod me again about it later and I'd end up telling her more.

By the time evening rolled around, the heat had died down. I still didn't hear the whir of the air conditioning but at least the temperature outside had cooled enough to be bearable.

I'd wanted to change into something lighter but only had a pair of pink athletic shorts I had from high school that were clean. I ended up keeping my work blouse on and tying my hair in a ponytail as I carried my dirty clothes to the laundry room located in the basement of our building.

As a precaution, I brought my necklace and hid the taser within the pile of clothes. If Marty decided to show up and hurt me, I could easily subdue him or at least keep him at a distance long enough for me to call the police. That's *if* he decided to hurt me. He'd hurt me in the past but I still didn't know why he was showing up at my doorstep now. Was he here to say he changed? Did he want us to try again? He hadn't left a message with Riley or given any reason for his surprise visit. He had just asked to see me. The mysterious circumstances worried me.

After putting two loads through the washer and dryer, I was relieved I didn't have to use the protection items. There hadn't been anymore Marty incidents since Monday and I was hoping it would stay that way. By the time I got back to the apartment with the last batch from the dryer, the air had cooled. It was still warm though and I brought a glass of ice water into my bedroom for refreshment as I folded my laundry on my bed.

Riley had moved from the couch to her room, following through with her plan to sleep early.

I'd just finished folding the last garment when my laptop chirped. A window popped up indicating there was a Skype video call from *V. Sorenson*. I took a seat at my desk and clicked "accept". Moments later, Vincent's stunning face appeared on my computer screen. He was thousands of miles away but now right in front of me. I missed his spicy scent but just seeing him still had a strong effect. Sometimes I hated technology for making my life more complicated—emails, social media, always being connected to work—but this time I loved it.

I turned the volume high enough to hear Vincent but not enough to wake up Riley in the next room. She was a heavy sleeper and I doubted even a blow horn would wake her.

Vincent was in a gray dress shirt without a tie and the top button undone. His face had a bit of evening stubble. The ruggedness contrasting with his elegant attire was startlingly attractive. He looked tired from a long day but seemed excited to see me.

I smiled at him. "Hey," I said cheerily.

"Hey," he responded with enthusiasm of his own. "Can you hear me? Is the video coming through?"

"Crystal clear. Your handsomeness is transmitting in its full high definition glory. Am I coming through for you?"

He smiled. "Yes, but nothing can compare to the real thing. How are you, Kristen?"

"Good, just finished some laundry. How about you? How's your trip going?"

"Not bad. Business as usual." He paused for a moment. "I've missed you."

I blushed. The words weren't unexpected but it was still surprising to hear them out loud. "I missed you too."

His dark eyes were scanning my surroundings. "You've got a nice bedroom. I like the stuffed animal in the background."

I laughed. I'd seen it so often, I'd forgotten it was there. I got up from the desk and went to retrieve the stuffed bird from my bed to give Vincent a better look at it. And an explanation for why a grown woman in her mid-twenties had a kid's toy.

"I also like those shorts," he said. "I couldn't agree more."

I turned back to Vincent. "What do you mean?"

"It says 'juicy' on the back."

"Oh God." My face heated. "I didn't have anything else to wear. I got these when I was in high school. A lot of girls wore them at the time and I caved to peer pressure. I should've thrown them out."

He grinned. "I'm glad you didn't. Suits you well."

Hoping to move on to a less embarrassing topic, I picked up my bird and brought it back to the desk. "On the other hand, I'm never going to throw this out."

"Why do you have a plush penguin?"

I squeezed the soft rainbow beak, posing its adorable face for Vincent. "It's a puffin. It looks like the offspring of a penguin and a parrot if they ever mated. I used to be obsessed with them when I was like five. My parents got me this during a trip to the museum. That was back when I had a better relationship with them. I'm not as into puffins now but this guy still has a lot of sentimental value."

"I can see why you like it. It's cute."

"Well I'm glad you and Mr. Waddles get along." I wiggled its nubby feet at Vincent. "His approval of you means a lot to me."

Vincent smiled in a way that was both charming and cute. If only I had a plush version of him to snuggle with on nights when he was away on business.

"Spunky on the outside, soft on the inside. You're quite the combination."

He continued as if another thought just occurred to him. "I know I've said this before. But thinking about you is making it difficult to concentrate on business. I don't expect you to understand but it's hard to focus on work when you've got an erection."

"Well. . . I don't know what to say." I really didn't because I'd never had an erection before but I could at least imagine the dilemma. I offered the first suggestion that came to mind. "Why don't you just watch porn like a regular guy?"

His brows knotted and his lips frowned. "Wouldn't work. You make porn look bad." He opened his mouth to say something further but closed his eyes and sighed deeply instead.

"Something's bothering you. What's wrong?" I asked.

His elbow on the desk, he ran a hand through his wavy hair but stopped halfway so that he rested the side of his head in his palm. He looked weary. "I wished we didn't have sex."

Nerves shot through my system and my grip on Mr. Waddles tightened. Why would he say such a terrible thing? Was it because I dumped my baggage on him and now he regretted being involved with me?

"What? Why?"

"Cause it made me want you more. I can't stop thinking about it. You in a blindfold. Your gorgeous body. . . It's so damn frustrating being so far away from you."

Relief washed over me like a cold shower in this summer weather. "You scared me for a second there. I thought you were going to say you didn't like the sex."

"I don't like *how much* I liked it. I'm dangerously close to cutting this trip short to come back to Manhattan. I'm not sure how much longer I can go. I think I might be addicted to you."

I felt his pain. Over the past two days, I'd constantly thought about him and our multiple sex sessions at his place. It had been distracting—something I welcomed given the drama of my ex lurking in the background; Vincent was a much needed diversion. But most of all, it made me realize how far I'd fallen for him in such a short time. It was frightening and thrilling—knowing he was feeling the same way about me made it less scary.

I had an idea.

"Maybe this will help," I said as I placed Mr. Waddles on the far end of the desk away from me. I released my hair from its ponytail and let my locks drape around my shoulders. I shook my head to give my hair the voluminous and sexy look I'd seen in commercials. Then I smiled seductively at him.

He straightened in his chair. "You have my attention."

I undid the top button of my shirt then the next two, enticing him with a view of my black bra beneath and an eyeful of scandalous cleavage. The nurturing side of me wanted to heal his pain.

"Mmmm," he murmured.

"Like what you see?" I teased. His desire for me always gave me a thrill.

He nodded slowly. "I want to see more."

I looked down at my chest. My breasts were nearly fully exposed. For some odd reason, I'd thought the ample skin I was already showing would be enough for him. But Vincent wasn't like any other men; I'd forgotten whose sex drive I was dealing with.

"I'm not sure," I said, hesitantly.

He smiled wickedly. "Let me see those gorgeous tits."

Showing cleavage was one thing, exposing full-on nipples was another. I couldn't help recalling a spate of stories in the media recently about a misbehaving senator sending naked pictures of himself to his mistress and those images getting leaked on the internet. I wasn't a senator, but I still had a reputation I needed to protect. The bad part of the internet was anything that got on there would be around forever.

I glanced at my door handle. Riley was likely in dream land and even if she wasn't, my door was still locked. I didn't know how safe it was on Vincent's end. "What if someone walks in on you? Or how do I know you're not recording this? I don't want my chest all over the internet."

"I'm in my hotel room right now. No one's coming in. Trust me, I'm not going to record this but every inch of your beautiful skin is going to be seared into my memory." His finger touched his temple. "I'm going to keep the image of your luscious breasts all to myself."

"I don't know. . . I'm not in the habit of doing internet camera shows. The idea makes me feel a little vulnerable."

His brows narrowed into sharp lines. I knew that look. It was the same one he got whenever he was in the middle of conducting serious business. He was thinking. Hard.

"Here, I'll expose myself. We'll both do it. I'm trusting you not to record this. I have a lot to lose if this gets out."

I thought about what the headlines would say: *Billionaire exposes penis to wealth manager. Cock grows while stock shrinks.*

Exposing himself was a huge risk for him, which demonstrated how much he wanted to see me naked. Even for a risk-taker like Vincent, I realized this kind of vulnerability meant a lot.

"Umm. . . okay I guess. You first," I said, unsure whether he was bluffing or serious. If he didn't do it, I wouldn't either.

The corners of his lips curved upward. "A dare? I usually go by 'ladies first' but you've given me something to work with so I'll make an exception."

He aimed the camera down to his lap, where I saw the front of his slacks tented. *He was hard already? Just from that small amount of skin I showed him?* My belly fluttered at the sight of the bulging fabric. Was he really going to do this?

I watched with bated breath as one of his hands gripped the black belt at his waist while the other tugged on the silver buckle to loosen the tightness. The leather arched into his palm and with a controlled jerk he drew two elegant prongs from their fitted holes. He pulled the tapered end of the belt through the rigid frame of the buckle, the band first being resistant but then sliding easily, yielding to the demand of his fingers. A few more inches, and the belt wrapping his powerfully trim waist was freed. He released the two separated ends and let them hang lazily in his lap. He wasn't exposed yet but I still felt the familiar tingles of excitement laced with arousal ripple through my body.

I marveled at how such a small gesture could inflame my senses. I wouldn't have believed it if not for the pulsing between my thighs reminding me how turned on I was becoming.

His hands were working quickly and my mind and body needed time to catch up with each titillating movement.

Once he unhooked the clasp on his slacks, he moved his fingers to his fly and paused.

"I know how you like it slow," he purred.

He slowly drew the zipper down and peeled the flaps of his pants back, exposing his dark boxer-briefs. Here it comes, I thought, my pulse beating quickly. He reached into the front opening, curled his fingers around the bulge hiding beneath, and pulled his cock into plain view. He released his hand and it stood erect on its own, the bulbous tip staring back at me, flushed with anger.

My hand flew to the base of my neck and my breath caught. How could a cock be so savage-looking and beautiful at once? And why was I getting so turned-on just by the sight of him?

I'd watched soft-core porn on a few occasions. While it was nice, it never became a habit. I didn't think the visual stimulation was strong enough. However, watching Vincent undress and touch himself could change that opinion.

He raised the camera back to his face. "Your turn, Kristen."

I gulped. He'd followed through on his part so now I had to. I started to wish the glass of water I'd brought to my bedroom had been spiked with alcohol. Prickles ran across my skin. Was it getting hotter in here again?

Nervously, my hands moved to the next button on my shirt and were preparing to undo it when he interrupted me.

"Do it on the bed."

Okay. . . sure. . .

Pliant to his command, I straightened from my chair and padded softly to the bed. I tried a few different seductive positions, but couldn't figure out one that I felt was both comfortable and sexy. I'd never done this before and it turned out to be harder than I anticipated. "How do you want me?"

"Kneel down on the bed with your knees apart. Straighten your hips. Don't sit back on your heels."

His instructions were oddly detailed and precise. I briefly wondered if he'd done this cyber-show thing before and if so, with who. But the impatience in his words didn't give me a lot of time to think, instead they spurred my actions. He knew what he wanted from me and I was eager to please him.

I unbuttoned the next button, then the next. I wasn't sure if I was doing it in an alluring way or not but I saw the desire in his face grow after each button was freed.

"You're so beautiful, Kristen," he said, as if reading my insecurity. "You have nothing to be self-conscious about. Everything you do is sexy."

Finally I pulled my blouse away from my chest and then off my shoulders, intending to slip the garment from my arms.

"Easy. Take your time," he said in a low rasp, eyes intense and unblinking. "Let me enjoy you."

I slowly finished removing my shirt and dropped it to the bed beside me. My pulse was beating rapidly and my stomach was a bundle of coils. I was still in the kneeling position he liked but now only in my bra and shorts. How far was this going to go?

"You're making me so hard, Kristen."

Wasn't he already hard? How could he be even harder? Curious to see my effect on him, I asked, "Can you show me?"

He aimed his camera downward and I saw his cock again. It was somehow firmer, longer, and more savage-looking than before. A faint trace of precum made the tip glisten. A surge of arousal ran through me.

He then adjusted the camera and scooted his chair backward so that both his face and lap were on screen.

"Can you see it? Can you see how hard you make me?" he growled. He brought one hand down to his lap and fisted his member. He began slowly stroking himself, eagerness making him forget to lube his palm. I was shocked he was masturbating in front of me. This wasn't just a camera show anymore; this was turning into cyber-sex. Fast.

I'd always thought the idea was silly—two people telling each other what they'd like to be doing to the other and each performing the action on themselves. It seemed more masturbation than sex, which didn't seem very appealing. But the deepening ache in my loins disagreed.

I'd never watched a guy jerk-off before and the sight of Vincent doing it, made me a little curious and a lot aroused. Although his strokes were slow and short, he was rougher with himself than I would be with him.

"I can see it."

"Touch your tits as I touch my cock. Make me harder."

Emboldened by the sight of his arousal, I began rubbing my breasts over the bra for him, pushing them up and squeezing them together in suggestive motions. It felt natural and sexy.

He grunted approval.

I reached across my chest and undid the clasp. I pulled the bra off and laid it gently on top of my blouse but covered my breasts with my hands.

"No hands, Kristen," he commanded, impatience and lust dripping from his voice.

I was getting into this, not just turned-on but also having fun. I was doing something risky I'd never done before and I was beginning to see the appeal. It was making me bold in a way I'd never expected. Having Vincent giving me orders for his pleasure made me want to do the same for him.

"You first, Vincent. No hands."

"What?" He continued pumping himself while drinking in the sight of me.

I wagged my finger playfully at him. "You heard me. No touching yourself until I say so."

His fist stopped its motions and he furled his brows. "Why?"

I smiled. "I want to tease you like you enjoy teasing me."

"Are you trying to kill me?"

My smile widened. "You're so melodramatic."

"Damn it Kristen, you can't expect me to watch you touching yourself and not allow me to jerk-off. That's like putting a bone in front of a dog and asking him to sit still. It's cruel."

I was amused by his analogy. The image of Vincent Sorenson on a leash at my beck and call certainly had its appeal. "Be a good boy and you'll get your reward. Okay?"

He grumbled then sighed heavily, his cock still hard as ever. "I don't like it. . . but fine. I'll do it for you."

"Thank you." Seeing him comply, I slowly removed my hands from across my chest, allowing my breasts to be fully exposed to the camera.

His jaw clenched and his cock twitched making me both fascinated and aroused by his male anatomy.

I began rubbing my breasts in circles, taking time to caress the hardened tips. I was feeling desirable from the yearning in his gaze.

Spotting the glass of water by my bedside, I reached over, pulled out an ice cube, and watched his eyes widen. The cold sensation between my fingers felt good in the warm air. I raised the cube to my chest and sucked in a deep breath when the cold touched my nipple. A surge of arousal heated my core and I squeezed my thighs together. I slowly circled the ice around the hardened tip, relishing the frigid bite on my fevered skin.

Vincent was chewing his bottom lip so hard I thought he'd draw blood. "You're so seductive, Kristen. I'd give my own two thumbs just to taste you."

He clenched his fists by his side, straining against the desire to touch himself. His discipline was admirable and his desperate desire was making me scorch.

"I want my tongue and mouth all over your breasts. I want to nibble gently on those hardened tits," he grunted. "Pinch them for me."

I placed the ice back in the glass and did as he asked, imagining Vincent's sinful mouth in place of my hands. Soft moans escaped my lips as I pinched my nipples and tweaked them a little roughly like I knew he would do if he were here. It was the perfect mix of pleasure and a slight edge of pain.

"You're doing so well," he said, voice straining with lust.

"So are you," I cooed, seeing his palms on his thighs, fingernails digging into the skin in resistance. His usual calm expression looked tortured.

"You don't know how difficult this is for me."

"Never had to wait for something you wanted?"

"Never wanted anything so damn much."

Still in the kneeling position Vincent liked, I slipped my fingers into the waistband of my shorts and slid both the shorts and the panties underneath down. I had to lean back to kick them off giving him a full view of myself, which I knew he appreciated. Fully naked before the camera, I resumed the familiar kneeling position.

"Your body's driving me insane."

"What would you do if you were here? Right now?"

"I'd use my tongue to take care of that throbbing clit of yours. It needs special attention."

I began rubbing easy circles around my clit with my fingers, imagining Vincent's expert tongue on that sensitive spot. "Feels good, Vincent."

"I can imagine it. The sweet taste of your cunt on my lips." He licked his lips decadently. "My mouth's watering just thinking about it. That's what you do to me, Kristen."

"Mmhmm. . . I like your mouth on me. It feels so good." I increased the pace of my fingers on my clit.

"You're so greedy. I see it in your eyes. I know you want more. Put two fingers inside yourself. That's my tongue burying inside you."

Without skipping a beat, I obeyed his command, thrusting two fingers into my wet, aching sex. "Ohhh, *Vincent*." My other hand began rubbing my breasts. It was as much for his pleasure as it was for mine.

I wasn't sure how long I was going to make him wait to pleasure himself. He looked like he was about to explode in more ways than one.

"You can touch yourself now, Vincent," I said, breaths uneven. "I think I've teased you long enough."

He gritted his teeth. "No. You need to come first. I have to see the look on your face when you come thinking about me. You're going to come first, then we're going to come together."

"Yes," I breathed, feeling my orgasm approaching dangerously fast. I hadn't even had one yet and he was telling me I was going to have two. I would've doubted my body could manage such a feat if Vincent hadn't made me come twice in quick succession Monday night. The idea of having two orgasms made my mind swirl and the pleasure from my fingers intensified.

I stared into his gaze, mesmerized by what I saw. He wasn't just drinking in my image with those intense brown eyes; he was ravaging me in his thoughts and I could almost feel it.

"I'm getting close, Vincent," I panted.

"I see it. Do it. But don't close your eyes. Watch me as I watch you come."

My fingers found a sensitive spot deep inside. They focused on that one area, increasing their pace as pleasure ripped through my body. I could feel myself approaching the edge fast, the force from Vincent's gaze pushing me to a perilous cliff.

"Oh God!" My hand gripped my breast as my orgasm slammed into me. I watched him through tear-filled eyes; watched his dark gaze burrow into mine, his pained expression turn desolate. I heard him release a strangled cry as a bead of semen erupted from the tip of his cock. I thought he would reach to shield it but his hands remained obediently on his thighs. Left untouched, the cum trickled along the underside of his erection. It wasn't a full release, but it was more than just precum.

It then occurred to me that he'd come without any touch—just the sight of me was enough.

"Jesus, Kristen. You see what you do to me? You see what you do to my god damn cock? You make me lose control."

Still a little blurry-eyed, I said, "I see it, Vincent. It's so hot. It's making me want to touch myself again." While still in my post-climax bliss, I began to rub my clit again. It was a little numb but it still felt good and the pleasure was getting better by the second.

He growled approval. "Don't stop. I'm going to touch myself now. I'm going to imagine that sweet cunt of yours wrapping around me tightly." He took his right hand and gathered the cum along the underside of his member and swirled it around the length of the shaft and the surface of the head for lubrication.

"This," he said holding up his hand, fingers together and half-way curled with thumb across the top, "Can't compare to you. But we're both going to use our imaginations. Watch yourself sit on my lap. "

He slowly brought the tunnel he made with his hand down to his lap where it hovered right above his erection. I watched with heated anticipation as the soft but firm opening gave a little as he slid his fist over the head, wrapping the girth tightly. The explicit image made my body recall how it felt to have him enter me for the first time. The size and fullness was mind-scrambling.

He wrapped his fingers around his member and began smoothly stroking himself while bucking his hips forward with each movement to penetrate the tight enclosure.

The detailed visual made it easier for me to imagine myself spread across his lap, eagerly bouncing up and down as I savored the delicious experience of being impaled by Vincent. I timed the thrusts of my fingers into myself with his strokes, making the situation seem more real.

As the pleasure grew, my knees began to fatigue so I leaned back, supporting my weight on one elbow with my legs spread wide.

"I like that position even better." He grinned.

He continued pumping his cock at an insistent but leisurely pace, both of us enjoying the physical pleasure and visual stimulation. Our breathing was stuttered and we were both sweating.

I was starting to feel a bit lightheaded from the heat and dizzying eroticism so I reached over to my nightstand to take a sip from my glass of water.

"Getting hot?" he growled.

"You know it," I panted, fingers still working inside my pussy. "Air conditioning broke earlier today."

"What if you took some of that water and poured it on yourself?"

I giggled at his distinctly male suggestion. "And get my bed all wet? I'm all for your creative ideas but I think that one's a little impractical. I don't want to sleep in soggy sheets."

"It combines my two favorite things. Water. And you."

"I'm sorry. What can I do to make it up to you?"

"Surprise me."

I thought about what else I could do to stimulate him. Then I remembered I had my vibrator in my nightstand. Nobody except Riley knew I had it but after seeing

Vincent pleasure himself, I felt comfortable showing it to him. I leaned over and pulled the smooth silver rod out.

I held it up for him. "This is smaller than you. But we'll both use our imaginations," I said, mimicking his words.

His pleasure-tortured expression became laced with fascination.

I switched the toy on and brought the buzzing tip to my entrance. Immediately, the vibrations on my sensitive folds surged through me, fueling my arousal. I used it to massage my clit for a little while then eager for a feeling of fullness, I thrust it inside myself. My head tilted back and I moaned. Cries of ecstasy escaped my throat, some coherent, some not, but I was sure I heard Vincent's name several times.

"I guess this means I win the bet," he said with dark lust, breaths heavy and fist pumping hard. Beads of sweat dotted his brows and a few strands of his wavy hair were matted to his cheeks. "You're masturbating while thinking about me."

"If you recall, I never took that bet," I replied, barely able to catch my breath or my mind for that matter. I licked my lips because all the moaning had made them dry. "And if I did, I would've lost anyway when you called my work phone that day."

"I knew it." His mouth curved into a wicked smile. "Your voice gets this tiny rasp when you're turned-on."

My face grew shamefully hot but embarrassment wasn't enough to stop my hands from shoving the vibrator in and out of myself. If anything, it fueled the heat burning in my core. "No it doesn't."

But then I heard it.

"Just like that." He laughed. Then abruptly groaned from the stimulation. "Just like that. . ." His voice trailed off in a whispered moan.

The erotic sound of his cries vibrated through me making me tremble and clench tighter around the silver cock inside me. Like before, I timed the thrusts of the toy with Vincent's strokes. The pleasure was stronger than it was when I was using my fingers and I could already feel myself approaching another climax.

"Come for me, Kristen. I'm right there with you."

Vincent's strokes grew frantic and urgent and so did my thrusts. It was just me before, but now we were both now edging toward a cliff.

"Kristen, you're making me lose it," he cried.

The vibrations from his voice combined with the vibrations from the toy drove me over the edge. "Vincent, I'm coming!"

"*Fuck Fuck Fuck.*"

Right before my world darkened, I saw him desperately try to cup the tip of his cock with his hand and semen bursting violently from the gaps between his fingers onto his lap and keyboard. He howled a choked cry of both pain and relief as my eyes rolled back into my head from my own orgasm. I heard his heavy panting and soft groans through my speakers as I laid on the bed, feeling like I couldn't move.

After a few minutes, he spoke. "Jesus, Kristen. I need to get a towel because of you. Maybe a new laptop."

I'd recovered enough energy to prop myself halfway up. My limbs still felt wobbly but I was eager to look at him. I smiled. "I'm sorry. I guess I owe you one."

"Don't be. I'd buy a new laptop every day if I could see you touching yourself."

"You're so sweet." I grinned.

"I don't think Mr. Waddles approves of me anymore after what I had you do."

I laughed and glanced at the plush puffin on my desk where I left him. Lifeless eyes hid recent trauma. "He'll get over it. I enjoyed it. You might say I found the experience thrilling."

Vincent winked at me then got up from his chair to grab a towel. I got a peek at his firm backside which made me consider going for round three, but my boneless body protested. I went to the bathroom and quickly washed up. Moments later, Vincent returned to the screen in his boxer-briefs and began cleaning up the evidence of our session.

"So have you done this before?" I asked as I tugged on fresh pajamas and took a seat at my desk. "You know, this whole cyber sex thing?"

"This was a first for me. I wouldn't take a risk like this unless it was worth it."

"You could've fooled me, it sounded like you knew exactly what you were doing."

"Sometimes you just follow your instincts," he said, smiling.

A yawn bubbled up to my mouth and I tried to stifle it with my hand.

"Are you going be able to sleep?" he asked. "I would've liked to be there to keep you warm, but unfortunately we're apart."

"I appreciate the thought but I don't think I'm going to have any trouble falling asleep tonight." My hand covered another yawn. "I think you wore me out."

"I told you I can be very demanding."

"If only I'd known what you meant back then at your office."

"Would you still have agreed to be my point-of-contact?"

The corners of my lips rose. "I would've thought twice if I knew I'd be masturbating on camera for you a few weeks later. I don't think I would've been so keen on that idea."

"It's a good thing you didn't know then." He gave a sly grin then continued. "I can see that you're tired. We'll have plenty of time to catch up this weekend."

I touched my fingers to my lips and then kissed the camera with it. "Night, Vincent."

"Goodnight, Kristen."

Chapter Four

After the intense video chat session the night before, Thursday was remarkably uneventful. Vincent had been tied up with business all day and night so we didn't Skype again. He said he'd make it up to me by taking me somewhere special this weekend. After flying on his private jet to St. Thomas, I could only imagine what "special" meant.

Friday rolled around and I was excited because Vincent was returning to Manhattan. I'd been busy with research on a new lead for Carl. It was a woman who had recently made a fortune from creating a shoe that could easily change from heels to flats. It was one of those genius ideas that makes you slap your forehead and say, "Why didn't I think of that?"

I didn't slap my forehead though, instead crinkled it as I diligently researched her background. If there's anything I've learned from my time with Vincent, it's that successful people win by playing by their own rules. I was too busy trying to follow other people's rules to make up my own. And I was okay with that, for now.

I looked at the extra duffel bag I had set next to my filing cabinet. This morning Vincent had texted me saying he was going to pick me up after work and I should pack a swimsuit and extra pair of clothes. It probably meant we were going somewhere tropical again. Of course, I didn't complain.

My eyes were on the clock on the lower right corner of the computer monitor, watching the last few minutes of the work day tick by painfully. I felt like a kid waiting for recess. In addition to the items Vincent asked me to bring, I packed something extra. Sexy lingerie.

I waited for him at the usual spot behind the office building as he pulled his Camry to the curb. I opened the passenger door and hopped in.

He smiled and I smiled. We locked eyes then locked lips in a passionate embrace. We both missed one another and the kiss said it better than words ever could.

"You ready?" he asked. He was wearing a t-shirt and khaki shorts like the first time I met him in Cape Town. I'd almost gotten used to seeing him in a dress clothes so the effect was striking. Definitely sexy casual.

"So ready."

He flicked the heart-shaped pendant around my neck. "I like how it looks on you."

I glanced down at it. The deadly weapon looked rather cute. It certainly matched my outfit. "I've gotten a few compliments so far. You have good taste."

We drove off and I settled into the feeling of being physically next to Vincent again. I watched the buildings and people pass by outside the window and periodically stole glances at Vincent's beautiful features.

"Not going to ask me where we're going this time?" He smirked.

"I figured it's somewhere with water. But I'm eager to be surprised."

"Seems like I'm rubbing off on you."

"Maybe." I grinned. "Although I'd much prefer you rubbing *on* me."

It was his turn to grin. "Don't worry. I assure you there will be plenty of that this weekend." He gently patted my thigh to console me.

Before long, we arrived at the airport and stepped out onto the familiar tarmac. Hand-in-hand, we boarded his private plane.

The pilot was the same middle-aged gentleman who flew the plane when we went to St. Thomas but this time there was also a flight attendant. She was an elderly woman who introduced herself as Nancy and ushered Vincent and me to a row of three seats in the rear cabin. We had rows of seats in front and back of us which provided a bit of privacy while the space between rows were big enough for ample leg room. After stowing away our bags, she took a seat at the front cabin near the cockpit, preparing for departure.

During take-off and twenty minutes into the flight, Vincent's hand seemed to never leave my leg, heating my thigh and running light touches along the skin with his fingertips.

My gaze was fixed out the window watching as the city below us became tinier. It was still hard to believe I was going for another weekend trip via private jet.

"Like the view?" Vincent asked as he caressed my thigh, his voice silk and his scent delicious.

"I like the feel as well," I said, eyeing his hand petting me.

"You remind me of a cat. Feisty at first but once you earn their affection they can be very receptive. Plus, you like birds."

"I'm flattered. Didn't figure you for a cat person though." I looked at him curiously. "Cats are great but I think I'm more of a dog lover. I had a yellow labrador when I was growing up. They're loyal, obedient, protective, always smiling at you." I touched the tip of his sharp nose with my finger and he smiled at me. "You remind me of a dog."

"I guess that's fair." His forearm rested over mine on the armrest and he began massaging the sensitive skin between my fingers with his own. "But don't expect me to hump your leg."

I laughed. "I wouldn't put it past you."

"I wouldn't put it past me either." He pinched the bottom edge of my gray pencil skirt. "Especially when you're wearing a skirt like this. I don't know what your bosses are thinking allowing you to wear something like this to work."

My face heated. "It's a typical work skirt, Vincent. Are you saying the dress standard for women in the professional world is unacceptable to you?" I teased. "Maybe they shouldn't allow men with your libido to go to work with women around."

"I don't care what other women wear. I care what you wear and if anyone else is thinking about these legs." He affectionately patted my thigh with his palm.

"Well then," I said, raising my brow at him. "You'll probably be pleased to hear my new client lead is a woman."

His hand on my leg tightened. "Only if you don't plan on pinching her nipples."

"Oh?" I said curiously. "I would've thought that would be a turn-on for a man with your sex drive."

"Turn it around. Have her pinch your nipples, then it'd be different."

I frowned. "How is that any different?"

"You'd be the one moaning."

Shock hit my system followed by a heated ache. Vincent was already a walking sex magnet but the time I spent apart from him made him like a sex vortex. This was going to be a long plane ride.

"Don't worry. The only client nipples I've pinched are yours and I plan to keep it that way."

"Hopefully it's not the last time you pinch them."

"So you like me pinching your nipples? I thought that was only something women liked to do and men were indifferent to."

"I like it. Gives me a charge."

I laughed. I could imagine most guys being embarrassed about admitting they enjoyed having their nipples tweaked but Vincent was very comfortable with his sexuality—at least in front of me. The confidence was alluring.

I lightly squeezed his nipple between my fingers and he made a soft groan. "You've opened my mind."

"Well maybe I can open you to other things as well. . ." His hand ventured between my thighs and began creeping up beneath my skirt.

I didn't resist but when his hand came dangerously close to my pussy, I nervously scanned the cabin. "Vincent, we don't have privacy. There's the pilot and the flight attendant at the front of the plane," I said, gesturing toward the cockpit. Peeking my head over the row of seats in front of us, I could see Nancy seated near the emergency exit reading a magazine.

"So?"

"So, I don't want to do anything that would embarrass us."

"I'm not embarrassed."

"You're not embarrassed if Nancy sees us—you know. . ."

"She has grandchildren." He leaned closer so that his lips were grazing my cheek while he spoke. "She knows what happens between two people when there's sexual attraction this intense." His hand slipped further up my skirt and brushed over my panties against my clit.

I desperately sucked air into my lungs to stop myself from moaning.

"Are you embarrassed? Of us?" he whispered.

My eyes darted to the front of the cabin. Nancy was still reading her magazine. "A little embarrassed of doing this in public. But I do like you touching me."

"Relax, Kristen," Vincent said softly. "We both know this flight is too long to go without us touching one another. We won't get caught if we're careful. We just have to keep quiet."

His hand found an opening in my panties and his fingers slipped inside. He ran one probing finger along my cleft, sliding up and down slowly. Insistent pressure fired raw nerves on sensitive flesh. I hadn't felt his touch in a week but the need was so great it felt like months.

I licked my lips.

"Just say the word, and I'll stop," he crooned. His finger found my entrance and dipped inside.

I bit my bottom lip. Stopping was the last thing I wanted. If anything, I was about ready to join the mile-high club.

I tried bucking against his fingers but the seat belt restrained my movements. Moving my hips forward gained slightly more penetration. But it wasn't enough.

Vincent kept his thrusts at the same depth.

"More," I breathed.

His thrusts became deeper and more insistent.

I tried stifling the moan threatening to burst from my throat but Vincent's hands were too confident, too skilled. I wasn't going to hold on. The last of my will broken, my fingers curled around the ends of the armrests. Eyes closed and head tilted back against the headrest, my mouth opened to scream.

Vincent's lips sealed over mine and I moaned into his mouth. His tongue dipped in, giving slow licks against my own, pacifying my quivering tongue.

The intercom buzzed. "Passengers, we're at our cruising altitude. You can remove your seatbelts now," the pilot said.

The lighted seat belt sign dinged then turned off.

I unbuckled myself and was preparing to thrust my hips into his hand when he grabbed me by the shoulder and spun me around so I was laying flat with my back across the row of seats. Before I could protest, he had my wrists restrained above my head with the seat belt straps. A position I was intimately familiar with since the night at his place.

With a grunt, he pulled off my skirt and panties along with it, discarding them beneath the seats in front of us. I gasped in horror, realizing that I'd never put them back on in time should someone stop by to check on us. They were as good as thrown out the emergency exit.

He dipped his head between my legs and went to work on my throbbing clit with his tongue. Soft flicks combined with fast and slow movements.

My breathing became rapid and shallow. I curled my toes and struggled against my wrist restraints, fighting off the cries of pleasure threatening to escape my mouth.

While his tongue continued firing sensitive nerves, he began thrusting his finger inside me. His slow back and forth thrusts became fast twisting and crooking motions. His fingertip found a delicious spot and I shuddered.

Next thing I knew, he placed his other hand on my pelvis below the belly button and pressed inward firmly. The pressure on that part of my body was unfamiliar.

"What are you doin—" I asked, but his actions answered before I could finish the question.

My hips instinctively curved upward under the force of his hand and his insistent fingers massaging a sensitive spot inside me hit a bullseye.

"Oh shit," I cried, pleasure tearing through my body. I closed my eyes and bit down hard on my lip to stifle another outburst. My hands fought against their restraints but it was deliciously futile.

How the hell did he do that? Vincent apparently knew my body better than even I did.

He gripped my thighs roughly and whispered gentle hushes into my pulsing clit. "Shh. . . quiet. . . so good," he groaned softly. Then he buried his face in my cleft, tongue penetrating my folds and nose rubbing my clit. He growled hungrily into my depths, tongue dipping in and out greedily, leaving no nerve untouched. "So fucking good," he bellowed, the low vibrations rumbling through me, making me clench all over to stop myself from shaking.

I was careening dangerously toward a second climax. Just a little more and he'd push me over the edge.

Then his tongue stopped.

"Keep going," I whispered fiercely.

He pulled his head up from between my legs and looked at me, wagging his finger. The gesture seemed oddly familiar. "Uh-uh."

My body was still hot and thrumming madly. "Please Vincent, I need release."

He smiled from leg to leg. "Payback, Kitten. For the Skype session. You'll have to wait."

I was too frustrated and horny to consider the implications of him calling me a pet name for the first time. He pulled away and I tried to rub my thighs together to finish what he started, but he caught my ankles with a firm grip. "Patience. I don't want you spoiling your need. I have a lot more pleasure for you tonight."

I groaned. I'd never wanted to climax more than I wanted to now. Never experienced the thrill of sex in public, of riding the edge of being caught and getting away with being bad. Never been driven to such desperate heights of pleasure. Never been denied the release raging in every bone in my body. And I never imagined uttering the words that were flying off the tip of my tongue. "I'm not a baby, Vincent. I know what my body needs. And it needs a thirty-thousand-feet-in-the-air sky-shattering orgasm right about now."

His expression softened. "I was too harsh. I left you too high. I'm sorry, Kristen. Let me help you come down slowly." He released my ankles and dipped his head back down between them. He gently tongued my clit and folds, easing the ache he had left there.

I moaned softly and closed my eyes at the delicious sensation.

A ding sounded and a light came on above our heads. I quickly realized I must've accidentally hit the flight attendant button with my hands. I heard Nancy close her magazine and begin walking toward the rear cabin. Panic swept through me. I was naked from the waist down and there would be no way I could pull my skirt and panties on in time even if I could slip my hands from my restraints.

Vincent moved from between my legs and casually reached into a drawer beneath the seat. Nancy rounded the row in front of us just as Vincent pulled a blanket over me, covering me from the waist down.

"How are you two doing? Can I get you anything?"

Vincent sat coolly in his seat, my feet resting on his lap beneath the blanket covering us.

"Kristen had to lie down because she's not feeling well. Do we have anything that'll make her feel better?"

"Oh my dear. Your face is all red. You look like you're burning up. I'll get you some water and motion sickness tablets."

"Thank you," I said, holding my hands behind my head, hoping my hair hid the fact that my wrists were bound together with seat belt straps.

By the time Nancy returned, I had slipped on my skirt and panties and sat back up.

"Oh you're looking better already. Here's the water and tablets."

I popped the tablets in my mouth despite not needing them and took a swig of water. "I'm feeling much better, thank you Nancy."

"My pleasure. Can I get you two anything else? More blankets?"

"We're good for now. Thank you," Vincent said. Nancy returned to her seat near the cockpit where she resumed reading her magazine.

Vincent turned over to me. "Who's the one not being careful now?"

"That was an accident."

"You going to make it until we land?" he asked, hand possessively caressing my thigh again.

"It's not like I have a choice do I? Unless I want to appear airsick again."

"It'll help if you try to get some sleep. I have a feeling you won't be getting much of that once we arrive at our destination."

Chapter Five

I managed to catch a light nap before we landed. Once the plane came to a stop, I stepped out into a cool breeze and seventy-degree weather. It was approaching evening but the sun was still out, illuminating the small airport and tropical scenery in the distance.

"We're on an island in the Caribbean called St. Lucia," Vincent said, hand at my back ushering me toward the terminal.

"Seems you're fond of the Caribbean."

"It's close to New York City where I spend a lot of my time nowadays. But this isn't our final destination."

This place seemed as good as any for an ideal weekend getaway. "Where are we going?"

"It's close by but we'll have to take a boat from here."

We hopped into a rented jeep and took a short drive to a harbor.

Vincent led us to a sleek boat with white hull and red trim. Letters along the side read "Pier Pleasure".

"Clever name," I commented.

He smiled. "Took me a while to come up with it. It was either that or 'Playbuoy'." He nudged me gently to indicate he was teasing.

"Glad you didn't choose the latter."

I didn't know anything about boats but I could tell it was built for speed. The controls didn't appear complicated— it wasn't much more than a throttle and a steering wheel—but the boat had a very big, very loud engine. The way we shot out as soon as I had put my life vest on and sat down next to Vincent told me handling this thing wasn't a job for amateurs.

He slowed the boat to a cruising pace as we headed off toward an island in the distance with the sun setting in the horizon casting red and orange hues on the deep blue waters. I wondered what he had in store for us tonight.

The boat came to a stop and he tied it to the dock jutting out from the shore.

"So what is this place?" I asked as I stepped off the boat onto the wooden planks.

"It's my private island."

"You own an entire island?"

"It's not that large, just a few miles in each direction. Not big enough for a runway. It's my personal spot to get away from everything."

First St. Thomas then St. Lucia. I was starting to see a pattern. "So what do you call it? St. Vincent?"

He laughed. "That's actually the name of a real island just south of here. The people on St Lucia call this place "île aux oiseaux", which is French for "Bird Island". There's a lot of pretty, exotic birds that live here."

"Interesting."

"Unfortunately, there aren't any puffins."

"That's a deal breaker," I teased.

His lips curved into a grin. "You're high maintenance. But worth it."

"I was just kidding," I said, playfully nudging him. "I really appreciate everything you've done. Surprising me on our dates. Being discreet, being supportive. I want you to know that all those things mean a lot to me."

His grin widened. "So have I changed your opinion about me?"

"What was my opinion before?"

"You tell me."

I sighed. "Okay, I'll admit I thought you were a bit of a sex-crazed playboy who was more hands-on with his recreation than with his business."

"And now?"

"The sex-crazed part hasn't changed."

"Maybe it has for you." He winked.

"Maybe," I mused. "I will say I've wanted sex a lot more in these last few weeks than in the past few years—possibly ever."

"Good, 'cause we'll be having plenty this weekend."

"Okay." I smiled. My response sounded a little odd to my own ears considering I'd rebuffed his sexual advances only weeks ago but a lot had changed since then. I had no intention of taking my response back.

He led us across the beach to a path leading into the forest. Fortunately I only packed a small bag so it was easy to carry, otherwise it'd be ridiculous rolling luggage across sand and dirt. After walking for fifteen minutes, tall trees swishing in the breeze and birds chirping all around us, we reached a small cabin with smoke billowing from the chimney. The setup reminded me of an old fairy tale involving bears—except my hair was brown. If I saw a bowl of porridge inside I'd probably make Vincent eat it.

He opened the door and gestured inside. "Ladies first."

I stepped inside and was hit with the spicy smell of wood. It was like the spicy scent I loved to smell on Vincent but stronger. The exterior looked rough but the interior was refined with smooth hardwood floors, elegant furniture, and a stone fireplace at the back that was already lighted. The cabin was small and cozy with various pictures and objects lining the shelves to each side of the fireplace. It felt more like a home than his condo in NYC.

"Quite a setup you have here," I said, admiring the surroundings.

"Welcome to my home." He dropped his bag on the brown couch in front of the fireplace and looked at me for my reaction.

"It's beautiful and quaint. Did you build it yourself?"

He laughed. "Although I would've liked to, it would've taken forever. I had it built a year ago when I purchased this island. I come here often but when I'm away, I have someone come by and maintain the place or prepare the place before I arrive."

"You sure know how to vacation."

I wanted to look around the cabin more, particularly at the pictures he had, but Vincent wrapped his arm around my shoulder and said, "Come on, it's getting dark. I want to show you something."

I put down my bag next to his on the couch and followed him out of the cabin. He led us further into the forest and we eventually popped out onto another beach. There was a tent set up with standing torches lighting the path around it. When we got closer, I could see it was some sort of Arabian-looking tent with lush reddish-lavender drapery. It was open on the side facing the ocean, giving a scenic view of the rolling waves along the shore and the small silhouette of other islands in the distance. Inside was a blanketed floor and a sea of cushions with middle-eastern-inspired geometric designs on them. There was a fire pit in the center and a hole in the roof above it.

"Private island, romantic tent—I can see how this would be a hit with the ladies."

"Since you're the first lady I've shown this place to, you tell me. Am I getting lucky tonight?"

"Unless you tell me this is all fake and I'm actually on some kind of twisted reality show, you are *definitely* getting lucky tonight."

"Not going to play coy?" He grinned. "I like how you know what you want."

We took a seat on the soft blankets and just as I was about to relax, my stomach growled.

Vincent laughed. "That's a familiar sound."

"I can't help it. Sometimes my body just does what it wants."

"You have an amazing body." He reached over to an ice chest and opened it to reveal an assortment of meats and veggies inside. "Let's feed it."

We cooked shish kabobs over the fire and ate to our stomachs' content. By the time we finished, the sun had gone down and only the dim glow of the moon and the torches nearby provided light.

"I'm stuffed," I said patting my belly.

"Any room for dessert?"

"Does it include blindfolds?"

He smiled and shook his head. Then he pulled out a bowl of strawberries from the cooler along with a bottle of chocolate syrup.

"Yum yum," I said, licking my lips. "Chocolate-covered strawberries are always a good choice."

He picked a plump one up by the stem and doused the tip in rich chocolate. "Open wide."

I closed my eyes and opened my mouth wide.

"You're closing your eyes, Kristen. You don't have to."

"I want to, though. You taught me to isolate sensations and I like that."

I could hear him smile. Then I felt the strawberry enter my mouth and I bit into the soft flesh.

"Mmm. So good," I murmured between chews.

We took turns feeding one another with strawberries and before long, we had finished the batch. Vincent put the bowl back in the cooler and said, "It's dark. We should head back to the cabin."

He twisted at the waist to reach for the cooler lid and I tugged on his outstretched leg. "Wait, there's something else I want for dessert."

He gave me a puzzled look as I crawled toward him. Snaking between his legs, I grabbed his waist and began unzipping his shorts.

"What are you doing?" he asked, as I pulled down his zipper and kissed the bottom row of his stone abs. The muscles beneath were hard but the surface of his skin was softer than I'd expected.

"I want to taste you, Vincent," I purred.

He gripped my shoulders firmly but gently. "We're out in the open. Someone might see us."

Fingers in the waistband of his boxer-briefs, I paused. "I thought you said we were alone on this island."

"We are. But we're exposed. Ships pass by here. Let's go back to the cabin."

I yanked his pants and underwear down, freeing the stiff erection I knew would be there. I playfully slapped his cock, causing it to wobble side to side and making him groan. "You're not afraid of having sex on your plane with a flight attendant twenty feet away but you're afraid of having sex on your private island with no one around. Gimme a break."

"It's riskier here. They could snap photos and it'll be in the tabloids. I don't want you to have to deal with that."

"It's dark. I doubt there are ships and even if there are, I doubt they'd see us." His cock rested heavily on his belly and I licked the underside from the base to the tip.

He groaned, the vibration making my nipples tighten. His hands around my shoulders constricted. "Your employers could find out if there are pictures," he said, voice strained.

"They won't."

"Let's just go—"

I took him into my mouth, sucking his heated flesh vigorously like the most decadent lollipop I'd ever tasted. He gasped and groaned painfully, growing harder by the second. I scarcely registered his hands moving from my shoulders to my hair, conveniently pulling strands away from my face as I went down on him; I was too busy enjoying the fierce throbbing sensation in my mouth. It wasn't the first time I'd given oral, but it was the first time I'd given it to Vincent and I wanted it to be memorable for both of us.

I began rolling my tongue over the tip as I sucked him greedily.

"Oh. No. Kristen," he cried, biting off the words.

I gripped his hips and pulled myself deeper then shallower then deeper again in a smooth cadence, enjoying the hard fullness of him in my mouth. Saliva covered his cock making it slick and harder to grip. My lips tightened, clenching him stronger and with more pressure, each milking stroke tighter than the previous.

Each of his male groans came more anguished than the last, turning me on intensely.

"*Fuck, Kristen,*" he snarled. "*Fuck it all.*"

His grip on my hair tightened and he began short hasty thrusts into my mouth, deeper than I had been taking him, but not far enough for me to gag. With his hand behind my head, gently guiding me and his hips pumping softly but urgently, I could feel him growing hotter, his need growing more desperate. The warm taste in my mouth became faintly salty, a distinct trace of his arousal. I thought he'd climax at any moment and I was ready to take him.

All of him.

He pulled me away, my lips making a popping sound when they released suction from his cock head. "I need to taste you," he growled.

In a frenzy of lust, he laid me on my back and tore off my shirt along with my skirt and panties, tossing everything behind him. Out of the corner of my eye, I saw my clothes accidentally land in the fire pit and burst into flames but heated lust overrode rational thought. If I had to walk around naked on Vincent's island, so be it.

Chest heaving, I spread my legs and he promptly positioned himself between them. He dipped his head and took one aching breast into his mouth, sucking and licking around the tip. He lightly pinched the tip between his teeth and pulled firmly. I gasped at the sensation, the ache in my chest traveling down between my thighs and making me clench my legs around his waist.

I saw him reach for the syrup and shake the bottle impatiently. He turned the nozzle upside down and began squirting chocolate across my chest. I gasped at the cool sensation. The first squiggles of chocolate were done haphazardly across my chest then he slowed down, making careful spirals around each tender breast. After putting the finishing touch on each tip, he cast the bottle aside and took a moment to admire his work.

With one finger, I swirled the chocolate around each tip, watching his eyes darken with lust.

His hands began plumping each breast. He dipped his head again and pulled one mound into his mouth, lapping up the chocolate, running long, easy licks along the syrup lines.

"Oh Vincent."

I arched my chest into him, relishing his hot mouth against my cool skin. He flicked the tender tip of my nipple with his tongue sending a heated shiver along my spine. I tilted my head back and moaned.

He ran patient but urgent kisses from my chest down to my thighs. Then he attacked my clit, flicking it with the tip of his tongue then lapping it with the full surface.

He lifted his head and pierced me with his dark gaze. "You've had this coming, Kristen," he growled. "You're too damn sexy."

Vincent reached into his pocket for a condom and quickly wrapped himself before his hips slammed into me at full force, penetrating me to the hilt, making me slide backwards on the blankets. I arched into him feeling too full and yet craving more at the same time. I watched the area where we were joined as he pulled back, every vicious inch sliding out, slick from my own wetness. I lifted my legs, spreading them further, encouraging him back to me. With only a primal grunt as warning, he drove forward again, entering me to the base, his balls slapping against my bottom. My fingernails dug into the sculpted flesh of his back and my teeth bit into the hard muscle of his chest. He cried wildly like an animal lost in heat.

"God, Kristen. You're too much."

I tried but couldn't form any coherent words. Only fervent moans tumbled from my trembling lips.

"I'm going to ravage you until our bodies can't move."

His filthy words sent me soaring; his thrusts sent me rolling like the waves on the shore. "Yes, Vincent," I cried desperately. "Take me. Take it all."

He pounded into me and I bucked into him. If a ship passed by and saw us, I didn't think I'd even care.

"I'm lost, Kristen. So. Fucking. Lost."

Passionate moans and painful cries filled the cool night air and the chatter of wildlife in the trees seemed to ebb and flow with the rhythm of our feverish bodies. We tumbled across a sea of blankets entwined at the hips, scattering pillows, chocolate syrup, and sand in every direction, making a mess of a carefully prepared arrangement.

The stars idly watched as we put on one hell of a show for them.

Chapter Six

I woke up in daylight surrounded by warmth. Every muscle in my body felt sore but in a good way. A familiar spicy scent tickled my nose and I realized Vincent was holding me in his arms tight against his chest, his calm breaths against the back of my shoulder and the morning breeze a feathery touch to my skin. Though no longer hard, he was still inside me. We were wrapped in layers of velvety blankets beneath a purplish-red roof under a dazzling blue sky. The fire in the pit had gone out. Was this another dream?

I shifted my naked body in his arms to face him and studied his stunning features. His dirty-blonde hair was disheveled. Traces of dry chocolate hung at the corner of his lip. I wiped it off with my finger and sucked the pad.

His eyes opened slowly, blinking a few times then revealing those dark irises I'd become so fond of.

"Hey," I said softly.

His lips curved up lazily. "Hey."

"It's morning."

He rubbed the drowsiness out of his eyes. "Did you sleep well?"

I nodded. I hadn't even remembered falling asleep. I couldn't remember ever being separated from Vincent's body last night. Had I fallen asleep with him inside me?

He yawned like a lion waking from slumber. "How do you feel?"

"Like I'd been thrown around by a tornado. You?"

He smiled. "Like I was in a fight with a panther." He twisted his head to look over his own shoulder. There were long red streaks marking his golden skin.

I gasped and began lightly massaging around the wounds, hoping it would help with the pain. "I'm sorry. I didn't realize I was scratching you."

"I didn't either." His lips gently kissed the tip of my nose. "Definitely feisty."

"I got carried away. I didn't know I had that side of me. I promise I'll be more careful."

He kissed my forehead. "That's going to be hard because I intend to bring that side out as much as I can."

"But I hurt you, Vincent."

He nuzzled his cheek against my head. "You make me feel alive."

I curled up into him, kissing his neck, inhaling his scent into my lungs. He was almost too good to be true.

"By the way, I'm sorry about your clothes," he said.

"It's all right. They were in the way. I won't miss them."

"We'll get you some new ones once we get back to the city."

"That sounds fun."

"Speaking of fun," he said. "I was thinking we'd explore the island today and do some birdwatching. You interested?"

I voiced my excitement for the activity, my adolescent interest in birds recently reignited.

After cuddling in front of the waves for a while, we decided to head back to the cabin. Vincent put his clothes back on and I had to make do with a blanket in place of the garments that had been destroyed in the heat of last night's passion. We rinsed up, put on fresh clothes, and ate a light breakfast of eggs and toast in the cabin.

I was perusing the pictures next to the fireplace while he went to find a set of binoculars. The first few seemed to be of him and his surfing buddies on various beaches across the world, grinning and showcasing their abs and surfboards. There were one or two women in the pictures but it was clear each was the significant other of one of Vincent's friends. A few other pictures showed Vincent shaking hands with famous people. It was obvious they were taken at events or parties. My eyes halted on a picture of just two people on a beach. It was Vincent smiling with his arm around a stunning brunette. Her straight silky hair framed sultry dark eyes and full lips. Her body in a bikini was elegant like a model's but she also had curves in all the right places. She was beautiful—much more so than me. My chest tightened with jealousy. Who was she? One of Vincent's ex-girlfriends?

Vincent returned to the living room with a pair of binoculars around his neck. "Found 'em."

"Great," I said. "Hey Vincent, who is this in this picture?"

He came to my side in front of the row of pictures. "Oh, that's Giselle, my younger sister."

Giselle. The name was pretty. I felt my chest relaxing, knowing she was Vincent's sibling.

Vincent had a sister? How come I didn't know that. Come to think of it, I didn't know much about his family even from all the research I'd done. There just wasn't a lot of information available. "I've seen a lot of pictures of you when I was researching your background. But how come I've never seen her in any of them?"

"Most of the pictures of me out there were taken when I was out in public. Some with my approval, some not. As you might've guessed by now, I like to keep my private life—well, private. That's why I was concerned about ships seeing us last night."

"Oh." I'd forgotten how famous Vincent was since our involvement. Our frequent interactions made him flesh and blood, real. It was easy to forget he was often under a watchful eye by the media.

"Your sister's very beautiful."

He paused, eyes seemingly far away, deep in thought. It was the same look he had when I first told him about Marty. "She's a good girl. I'd like you to meet her sometime. I'm sure you two would get along well."

I wondered what Giselle was like. Was she basically a female version of Vincent? Perfect and charming?

"Come on. Let's do some spying." Vincent put his arm around my shoulders and we headed out into the forest like a pair of adventurers.

The rest of the morning passed in a flurry of bird sightings—ones I'd never seen before or seen only in nature magazines. Vincent played tour guide, giving me details about the different species on his island. We traded off on the binoculars and I whipped out my phone periodically to take pictures.

We were hiding behind a bush, the sun bright overhead, when I spotted a familiar bird perched on a tree branch. "Whoa, that looks like a puffin but with a big 'ole beak."

Vincent laughed. "It's a toucan. Like the bird from those Fruit Loops commercials. Except this one is a Keel-billed Toucan."

We watched it groom itself, using its beak to preen its breast feathers. With its brightly colored coat and distinctively shaped head, it looked majestic.

Vincent pointed and I saw another bird on a branch behind the grooming one that looked to be of the same species but considerably larger. The big one was closely watching the smaller one, bobbing its head up and down, shifting from side to side on the branch inspecting the smaller one from every angle. The grooming one didn't seem to notice the sketchy behavior.

"What's that bird doing?" I whispered.

"The one grooming is female and the other is male."

The female toucan continued going about her business while the male silently hopped from branch to branch, edging closer to the female without her noticing. The female turned her head to preen at the feathers on her back and I thought she'd spot the male, but the male cleverly jumped to another branch out of sight as if anticipating her movements. Before long, the male made it to the same branch as the female, inched closer, then suddenly jumped on top of her. The female squealed and fluttered her wings but the male kept her steady with his strong claws.

"Whoa," I said, my finger clicking the shutter on my cell phone camera. "Is that big bird humping the little one?"

"It's called a cloacal kiss," he said. "Birds have an orifice on their backside called a cloaca for reproduction. They touch their cloacae together and the male deposits sperm into the female. In some species, it only takes a few seconds."

"Sounds kind of anticlimactic," I mused, snapping another picture.

"I guess it depends on the birds. I'm sure it's that way with some humans as well." He grinned.

"Not with us. It's a very long and hard process." I turned my camera to snap a picture of him.

He smiled. "With lots of climaxes."

"For sure. At least on the female's end."

"The female is what's important. The male has to win her over."

"Like some kind of challenge?"

He shook his head. "Because she's worth the pursuit."

"You could always try sneaking up and mounting the female like the birds do." I pointed to the toucans. The female had calmed down and become receptive to the male humping her.

"You think that would work?"

I smiled mischievously at him. "Catch me and find out."

He wrapped his arms around my waist and I playfully struggled to get free though I knew it was futile. "I got you."

"No fair," I said. "You have to give me a head start. Close your eyes and count to a hundred."

"There's steep slopes and sharp rocks on this island. I don't want you getting hurt."

"You're sweet, Vincent. But I think my fragile female body can handle a frolick in the woods."

"Okay, Kitten." He smiled, releasing his hold on me. "I'm game." He cupped his hands over his eyes then started counting.

I dashed off, zipping through the dense trees and hurdling over small bushes. I could hear the sound of his numbers growing distant.

"One hundred," he said, voice faint. "Here I come."

A few minutes later, I heard his footsteps crunching against leaves nearby and I ducked behind a large brush. I thought he'd find me but he walked right past the brush, calling out my name. I picked up a small branch from the ground and threw it in a different direction. He headed off toward the sound of the branch thumping against the ground and I had to keep my hand against my mouth to stop myself from laughing. I was amused I could outsmart billionaire Vincent Sorenson.

Once he was out of sight, I made my getaway in the opposite direction. I was having fun eluding him. I hadn't played coy last night, but today was different.

I'd planned on setting out in one direction but a series of large trees and shrubberies caused me to make several small, winding detours. After a while, I wasn't sure if I was still going in the same direction. Eventually, I realized I had no idea where I was going. I started to head back the way I came but stopped at a large scraggly tree, it's branches resembling gnarled tentacles—the distinct appearance was very memorable. If I was tracing back my steps, I should've spotted this tree before. Why hadn't I seen it before? Where was I? Vincent had said this island wasn't large but it seemed pretty big. I couldn't get a decent sense of my bearings because the thick foliage prevented seeing very far. I was starting to suspect I was lost.

I heard a rushing sound in the distance and having no better option, decided to track down its origin.

I came into a clearing and realized I was staring at the base of a waterfall. Water rushed from fifty feet high down to a large basin below that streamed out in rivulets to what I imagined was the Caribbean Sea at some point.

In awe, I stepped closer and perched on a smooth rock beside the edge of the pool and stared at the clear water below. There were a few colorful fish swimming that resembled Koi but smaller. I got on all fours and bent low to dip my hand in the water to try to touch one of them.

"Nice view," a voice said behind me.

Huh?

Strong hands gripped my waist from behind and a hard surface bumped into my backside.

I gasped and nearly fell into the water but the hands kept me stabilized. I twisted my neck to see Vincent behind me, his hips flush against my buttocks.

"You found me," I cried.

He smiled. "If you're ever lost, I'll find you."

Eager for a dip in the cool water, I pulled off my shirt and the rest of my clothes. "You haven't caught me yet," I said, jumping into the water nude to swim away from him. The basin was shallower than I expected because I was able to touch the floor with my toes when the water reached my nose.

Mischievous smile on his face, he removed his own clothes and cannonballed in after me.

I swam toward the base of the waterfall and almost made it there when Vincent caught up to me. He gripped my waist and turned my body to face him then he kissed me deeply.

Laughing and smiling, we swam to the base of the waterfall and behind it. There was a small enclosure in the rock like a shallow cave, large enough to comfortably fit two wet bodies. Vincent picked me up out of the water and sat me on the smooth stone ledge then gripped the edge beside me and pulled himself up.

"This is a hidden spot on my island," he said, the steady sound of water splashing in front of us. "You'd almost found it on your own."

"Are you secretly a pirate? And you keep your treasure back here?"

He raised his hand to my face and brushed his fingertips along my cheek. "You're my treasure."

I blushed. "You're always so smooth," I said softly. I reached to brush a wet strand away from his eyes so I could better appreciate the full handsomeness of his features.

His dark gaze intensified and his voice lowered intimately. "I may not be a pirate, but I'd still like to plunder your booty."

"Wow. So corny." I laughed. "I think I might have to take back what I just said."

"Couldn't help it. You made it too easy." He grinned. "But seriously, you have a very nice bottom." His hand reached around my waist to cup the back of my thigh and I leaned backward against the cold stone and lifted my leg to allow him to cup my buttocks. The stone was hard, but the position was comfortable.

"I guess that answers that then," I said.

He positioned himself between my legs and shifted over me, nipple rings dangling above my breasts. Water trickled down his bare torso forming droplets at the base of his abs that fell onto my sex. "Answers what?"

"The question of whether you're an 'ass' guy or a 'tits' guy."

"Why does it have to be one or the other? I like both. And everything around and in between."

I shrugged. "Don't ask me. I don't make the rules."

He squeezed my butt cheek and his lips curved upward. "Then let me show you how I break them."

He tilted his head and his mouth sealed over mine. His tongue slipped inside running long leisurely licks along my own tongue.

I could feel his thick member growing warm and stiffening against my thigh. My sex responded in its own way.

He brushed my wet hair away from my forehead and planted his lips there. "I like your head. It's beautiful, smart, and has wonderful thoughts."

"I'm flattered," I hummed. The water crashing around us contrasted sharply with the coziness of this little cave.

He moved slightly lower. I closed my eyes and felt his supple lips delicately kiss my eyelid. "Your eyes. Vivid and sharp."

I murmured approval, enjoying the tender words and intimate gesture.

He kissed my mouth again. "Your lips. Soft and firm."

My breathing quickened and I could feel my body throb against the wet stone.

He moved to my chest, sucking tender flesh into his mouth causing me to arch my back and moan softly. "Your breasts. Shapely and alluring."

I reached to tenderly touch his cheek and he kissed my hand. "Your hands. Warm and gentle."

He trailed light kisses down to my bellybutton. "Your stomach. Grumbles when it's hungry."

I giggled.

Then his head went between my legs. "Your cunt. Sweet and greedy." He kissed my clitoris then flicked his tongue rapidly against it. I exhaled deeply and licked my lips. Vincent was an expert at oral stimulation and I'd welcome his mouth there any day.

I thought he'd remain there but he pushed my legs back with his hands and went even lower.

His lips kissed at sensitive skin and I puckered at the sensation. "Your ass. Round and juicy."

Then I felt something soft and moist nudging the entrance. It was unexpected and I didn't have time to prepare myself. "What are you doing, Vincent? I've never—Oh!"

His tongue brushed light circles around the rim, wetting the entrance with his saliva. I'd never tried anything back there before not even on my own. I'd been curious but I was too afraid it would hurt.

"*Vincent*," I breathed, unsure if I wanted him to continue despite the pleasure rippling from where his tongue contacted my skin.

"Relax, Kitten. I've got you."

I wiggled my legs and tightened my core as Vincent steadily explored my bottom with his tongue and lips. Eventually, I finally relaxed. That's when his tongue was able to slip inside. His finger entered my pussy at the same time and I crossed my legs together tightly to control the pleasure. My feet found the low-hanging roof of the cave and I was able to press my toes against it to keep my legs up.

"Feels too good," I moaned. I bucked my pelvis into his finger and into his tongue. Each movement left me feeling full on one end and empty in the other. The seesawing pleasure coursing through my body was driving me over the edge. My hips became more desperate, my cries of lust more profane.

"You're making me so hard," he grunted.

He added another finger into my pussy and rammed me faster. I shattered on the rocks like the water crashing around us. My feet lost their grip on the roof and my legs came down, resting on Vincent's sculpted shoulders.

"I want you inside me, Vincent," I panted, eager for that feeling of fullness only he could give me.

He frowned. "We have to go back to the cabin. I didn't bring any protection with me."

I swallowed hard before speaking. "I'm clean, Vincent. Are you?"

His brows narrowed. "Yes but—"

"I trust you. I'm on the pill. Do you trust me?"

His eyes lit. "Yes."

"Then let's do it. Here. Right now."

"Are you sure? I want this Kristen, but I don't want you to have regrets."

I nodded. "I'm sure. I want this. I want to feel you inside me with nothing separating us."

"Oh Kristen."

He tilted his head and sealed his mouth over mine.

I reached for his erection—which was as hard as the stone against my back—and used the swollen tip to rub against my clitoris. He groaned into my mouth.

I aligned the tip with my entrance and he slowly entered, allowing me to savor the feeling of every bare inch spreading my throbbing sex. Deeper he dove, stretching sensitive flesh, firing raw nerves in his wake, leaving me mindless and breathless.

"You feel so good," he cried, his mouth trembling by my ear.

His thrusts were so deep. My body felt impossibly full. I gripped the muscles of his back tightly but careful not to scratch him with my fingernails this time. "Vincent, you're so hot inside me."

"I can feel my blood rushing," he groaned. "It's because of you, Kristen."

Our bodies were so close, his hard pecs flat against my breasts. I could feel his heartbeat through his chest, the strong beats vibrating through me, making my own chest beat harder. "I want you so bad it hurts. Don't stop."

He drove into me. Again and again. Shaky breaths escaping both our lips each time he hit the back of my sex. "I can't stop."

Our wet bodies collided over and over again. Our mouths and tongues twisted and tangled in clashing harmony. He plundered my depths and took what he wanted. I opened myself and gave him everything he desired, lost in senseless pleasure.

His thrusts became more urgent, his expression more desperate.

"I'm coming, Kristen," he groaned painfully.

"Come inside me, Vincent." I dared him with my hips and coaxed him with my fingers digging into his firm backside.

"Oh fuck!"

A wave of heat seared my insides as I felt him violently spurt inside me, filling me to a depth I'd never felt before both physically and emotionally. He continued pumping his hips, shouting curses, emptying more of himself. I clenched around him, squeezing every last drop of desire out of him and into me. I wanted him. All of him.

He collapsed on top of me, panting, surrendering. I enjoyed the feel of his weight against me, crushing me tenderly.

**

Once we were back at the cabin, we decided to take Vincent's boat over to St. Lucia to grab lunch and basic supplies for the cabin. After our morning activities, I was as relaxed and happy as I could remember. Being with Vincent was both comfortable and exciting at the same time. I could scarcely believe how well things were working out between us.

We walked from the cabin to the beach and boarded the *Pier Pleasure*. He was wearing a light blue linen shirt with the top few buttons unbuttoned and gray shorts of a similar fabric, with flip flops and Oakley sunglasses completing the look.

Untying the boat from the dock, the muscles in his arms and chest bulged beneath his shirt. More and more, watching him do any physical activity made me think of the way he looked naked.

After starting the engine, Vincent directed us on a beeline straight for the main island. He looked confident and collected piloting the boat, taking the waves in stride. As the wind and ocean spray blew through his wavy blond hair, he resembled something out of a movie. His face radiated focused intensity directed toward the task at hand; he was soaking this experience in and making sure we didn't have any mishaps.

For all that, I was white-knuckled next to him. He hadn't gone this fast our first time, and it felt pretty close to out of control to me. This was worse than a New York City taxi. I didn't know how fast we were going but it felt like a hundred miles per hour easy.

I had to ask. "How fast are we going?" I yelled over the wind.

Rather than respond immediately, Vincent gave the wheel a sharp turn. I screamed as the boat veered to the left and rolled in the same direction. For a second I thought the boat would flip, but it stabilized, and I was surprised at how exhilarated I felt as I settled into feeling the movement. Before we had even completed a circle, I realized I was having fun. Vincent's addiction to this kind of adrenaline rush was making more sense the longer I knew him.

Once we were pointed back at the island, Vincent eased the throttle down to almost nothing. "What did you say?" he asked, smiling.

It took me a minute to remember what that question had even been. "How fast was the boat going earlier?"

He shrugged. "Probably forty or so. I wasn't paying close attention. Nothing too crazy."

I had driven at a higher speed on the highway, but traveling on the water felt much faster than going a similar speed on land. "It felt crazy to me."

"Have you done much boating before?"

I shook my head. "Nope."

He nodded. "It's like a lot of things. At first it seems totally out of control, but most things that seem dangerous usually aren't too bad when you're with someone who knows what they're doing. Fact is, you'd have to be a really bad driver to flip this boat in these conditions."

"And you know what you're doing?"

"Most of the time, anyway."

As I wondered what *that* meant, he kicked the throttle up, and the boat raced off toward the main island.

I didn't know anything about boats, but even I could tell Vincent's was the nicest by far out of the half dozen I saw in the small marina we navigated into. The water was clear down to the sand below as we walked down the long pier to the beach. I could even see some fish congregating around the wooden pillars of the pier. A few dozen people were milling around the strip; it contained a single restaurant, a general store, a surf shop, and not a lot else. Past the palm trees and vegetation there were some houses further inland, and the occasional car or truck drifted by.

The warmth of the white sand between my toes was a pleasurable contrast to the ocean spray moments earlier. Vincent seemed to be surveying the beach as we stepped off the pier, but after a moment he turned to me.

"I hope you like seafood," he said, "because that's all there is to eat here."

I looked around. "I'm guessing it's fresh."

He smiled. "Just caught. Let's grab a table."

We walked over to the restaurant, *Isabela & Antonio*, and took a seat at one of the two tables on the covered patio. The establishment was owned by a husband and wife, both of whom were in their fifties and appeared to live on the second story of the building. Isabela took our order: I got the mahi mahi with mango salsa and Vincent asked for peppercorn crusted swordfish.

"Do you eat here often when you're down on your island?" I asked, once she had gone back to the kitchen.

Vincent nodded. "Antonio keeps it simple, but he's a great cook, and you can't beat the quality of the fish. I also buy from the local fisherman and cook myself at the cabin, but I like to support them any time I come over."

"It doesn't look like they have much competition."

He looked back toward the kitchen. "That's true, but people here tend to take pride in their work for its own sake, especially people like those two who weren't born here. You don't try to make a life in a place this remote because you're lazy, that's for sure."

I knew enough about Vincent's background to know he valued people who worked hard. You didn't get to where he had gotten without that kind of work ethic. I was the same way, though I wasn't quite as adventurous about going out on my own. "So far you've had very good taste. I'm excited."

He smirked. "Good. I like it when you're excited."

I blushed. He had been showing his affection a lot lately. "I'll bet. So how long have you been coming down here?"

"Years and years. I was coming here way before I bought the island. Surfing is good on the other side of the island. Too calm on this side."

Calm was good from my perspective. "I like this beach."

"Sure, and the conditions on the water are usually great for the boat."

"You're always looking for a little extra excitement, aren't you?"

"Usually. Not so much since I met you, though. You're a handful."

I laughed.

A minute later, our food came. Vincent was right: the preparation was simple but the ingredients spoke for themselves, which was the opposite of a lot of the food at restaurants in New York. I hadn't realized how hungry I was after our morning activities, but as soon as I smelled my food I realized I was starving. We both inhaled our meals. Isabela came with the check, Vincent paid, and we were soon making our way to the convenience store.

"We just have to pick up some odds and ends for the cabin," he said. "It's hard to get used to not having the basic necessities right around the corner when you're used to the city, but around here you have to."

I shrugged, contemplating the food in my belly. I wasn't ready to get back on that boat just yet. "No problem. I bet you're already thinking about flying around in your boat."

"I'm thinking about doing something in the boat, that's for sure." He winked.

My cheeks warmed. Could he really be in the mood again after yesterday and this morning? We'd certainly be exposed on the boat. But the rocking from the waves would be an interesting element. At this point, I knew if he came onto me, I would probably end up going along with it. He hadn't been wrong when it came to finding ways to pleasure me so far. I was still contemplating as we walked into the store.

The general store was surprisingly packed with merchandise, all at an eye-popping markup. When you're the only store in town, I guess you can charge what you want. Vincent picked out some toiletries and other necessities while I followed behind. He was a very efficient shopper. Within minutes we were at the checkout line. I was spacing out musing on the color labels of the liquor collection behind the counter—there was a very heavy rum focus—when a stunning blonde woman came in wearing a red bikini and stopped at the edge of the counter.

She had long, wet blonde hair and the definition of a beach tan—there was even sand still clinging to her torso. She had ample breasts, curvy hips, and a flawless complexion. Her six pack was so defined I wondered whether she was a fitness model. In fact, the more that I looked at her, the more I thought she must be an athlete of some kind.

When I turned my attention back to the counter, I saw the effect she was having on the men in the store, the clerk behind the counter included.

And Vincent. He turned his attention toward her like a shark smelling blood.

Jealousy stirred in my stomach. Working at a desk in the city didn't exactly let me compete on the body front with a woman like that.

The man at the counter cleared his throat. I thought he was going to point out some version of "no shirt, no shoes, no service," but he just said, "Hello, Ariel."

She had a model's smile, and she used it here. "Hello, Emilio."

Then she caught a glimpse of Vincent and beamed. "Vinny! Oh my gosh, you're here."

"Ariel, what a surprise." He smiled.

"I can't wait to straddle your newest board." She laughed.

Vincent shifted. "You'll have to let me know what you think. What are you doing in St. Lucia?"

She pushed her hair back over her shoulder and tossed her head. Every movement she made irked me. "*Surfing* is doing a photoshoot on this side of the island. You know, because of the sand. Not that I need to remind you how nice the sand is over here." She winked.

I looked up at Vincent's face. He appeared slightly flustered and he averted his gaze. Calm and collected Vincent losing his composure? How could she have such an effect on him? My jealousy worsened.

Ms. Photoshoot stepped closer to Vincent. I put my arm around his waist to remind him that I was still here. It made me angry he was ignoring me in front of this gorgeous woman. Didn't he realize he was making me jealous?

Vincent shook his head as if he were in a trance. "Sorry, bad manners. Ariel, this is Kristen. Kristen, this is Ariel Diamond."

He didn't even introduce me as his girlfriend. Reeling, I felt I should speak. "So are you a model?"

Ariel laughed in a way I found patronizing. "I'm mostly a surfer, but I do some modeling work, as well as riding Vincent's board every chance he gives me." She turned head and shoulders toward Vincent, as if I didn't exist. "Which, again, hasn't been enough lately, Vinny. When am I getting my personalized new toy."

He laughed. "I'll look into making sure you get it when I get back to work."

Another perfect smile tore its way through my ego. Who was this woman that was expecting a personalized surfboard from Vincent's company? Did she and Vincent have some kind of past he hadn't told me about? She was acting super familiar with him, and he wasn't shy around her either.

"Good," Ariel said. "Done any surfing lately? Or have you been hunkered down in that awful office of yours?"

My mind recalled the surfing lessons Vincent had given me on our first date. I hadn't been very good, but it had still been a fun day, especially in the showers afterward. That had been an important day for our relationship.

"Not really. We'll have to get together some time to do it properly."

I couldn't believe this.

Ariel continued. "Good, I'm holding you to it. You're always so much fun. Anyway, I have to get back to the set soon. Let me know about that board."

"Will do."

She left us to finish her shopping and Vincent checked out while I continued feeling invisible. It was unbelievable how small he'd made me feel. The way he interacted with Ariel made it seem like he didn't want me there. There were some ways I just didn't fit into Vincent's lifestyle, and one of those was doing extreme sports activities he loved.

We were both quiet on the walk back to the boat. I wondered whether I would ever be enough for Vincent.

We were barely into our relationship—or whatever it was we were doing—and already I was seeing holes.

As he untied our boat, his shirt slipped exposing more of his torso, including his diamond tattoo. It couldn't be a coincidence the symbol coincided with Ariel's last name. Was that for her? I decided I needed to ask him about his relationship with her, whatever that was, but the boat ride back to his island wasn't the place to do it. As the wind blew against my face, I thought about how I was going to broach the subject.

Chapter Seven

By the time we returned to the cabin and unpacked the items we bought, it was almost four o'clock. Vincent and I spoke little from the time we left the dock until we had finished putting away supplies. He seemed distant in a way he hadn't been since we'd been seeing each other, and it worried me. I took a seat at the dining table as he was beginning to busy himself in the kitchen.

"Vincent. We need to talk."

He looked up from the vegetables he was chopping and squinted. "Is something wrong?"

His obliviousness was amazing. The anger that had been bubbling up under my skin was ready to spill over. "That wasn't okay."

"What wasn't?"

"Don't play dumb. Every second you were talking to Ariel Diamond you were wishing I wasn't there."

Vincent took a deep breath, put down his knife, and sat next to me at the table. "That's not true. I'm very glad you're here."

I crossed my arms. There was no way he was getting off easy on this one. "Don't try and smooth talk your way out of this. Who is she?"

"She told you, she's a surfer. She's a world-class surfer, actually. Big name in the industry."

"Okay. And?"

"My company sends her free products for testing and endorsement. So that's what you heard when she was talking about sending her the new board."

"Okay, that explains that. How about 'Vinny?'"

He said nothing. His thousand yard stare reminded me of the way he looked in the store.

"Well?"

"You're getting way too upset about this."

I hated the way he was deflecting. The more he stalled, the more I realized something was up. "Am I? Have you had sex with her?"

He flinched. "Why would that matter?"

"Because I'm asking. You have, haven't you? Why didn't you tell me?"

He threw his hands up. "Because it's not important! Do you really want me to run down a list of every woman I've ever slept with?"

Thinking about the length of that list made me nauseous. I was sure he had slept with many, many more people than I had. Still, that wasn't what this was about. "No, I'd rather not think about that. But were you going to wait for me to bring it up before you told me anything about your relationship with her?"

His jaw worked, but he remained silent. I could tell he was going through the options of what to say in his mind. After several minutes of waiting for him to speak, I felt like I needed to move the conversation along.

"Okay, you're clearly not being forthcoming about this, so I'm just going to ask you: is the diamond tattoo on your chest for Ariel? Or is that just a weird coincidence?"

His mouth formed a thin line. He took several deep breaths, then put his hand on the table. "I should start at the beginning: it makes me feel old to say this, but I've known Ariel Diamond for thirteen years. Since I was a teenager."

I nodded. That was longer than I had known anyone except my parents.

He watched me for a minute, but I wasn't saying anything. He continued. "We met while I was in college. She was part of the crew I surfed with in California while I was in school and then after. You could say we kind of came up together. So I've known her for her whole career, and she's known me for mine."

"And you guys dated?"

He nodded. "Yes. Eventually we started dating. I got the tattoo for her when I was twenty."

"How long did you date?"

"A few years. It was up and down. We aren't really compatible, though I fought against that at the time. The only thing we really have together is surfing."

"So you loved her?"

"I definitely thought so at the time."

The next question was one I wasn't sure I would get an honest answer to. "Do you still love her?"

He shook his head firmly. "No. We still have a friendship, but I moved on a long time ago."

I had my doubts. He had a tattoo devoted to the woman. She was more than just a flame he had moved on from. "Really? Why didn't you get the tattoo removed?"

"Why would I? It's not like I'm on bad terms with her. We're just not right for each other as romantic partners. That doesn't mean we can't be friends."

I thought about my only real ex. Marty. We weren't exactly on the best of terms. The idea of being friends with someone you were once romantic with seemed pretty foreign to me, but it worked for some people. "So when was the last time you guys were intimate?"

He shrugged. "I don't know, five or six years?"

The way he was so casual about sex was often a turn-on, but right now it made me feel pretty insignificant. I had to keep the conversation going or I knew I'd dwell on it. "So all that innuendo from her was just joking around?"

"She was probably trying to get a rise out of you. I'm sure she knew we were together so she was probably testing you by seeing how you would react if she flirted with me."

Did he just say we were together? It didn't feel like it, especially after he'd let Ariel test me like that. Did I want to be with someone who would let me squirm?

"Are we together? Because I felt invisible while you were talking to Ariel, and it's even worse if you were conscious of the fact she was trying to do that."

His eyebrows shot up. "Felt invisible?"

"Please. You didn't even introduce me as your girlfriend." Granted, I wasn't sure whether I was his girlfriend. We hadn't talked about what our status was as a couple, or even if we were a couple.

He let out a deep breath and grimaced. "Sorry, that was an oversight. I was surprised and not really thinking."

That was a non-answer. "But you knew she was testing me and you just let her keep going. Why did you do that?"

"What did you want me to do? The way she was doing it, I would've had to say something very awkward and it would've made things uncomfortable for everyone. What she was doing was pretty harmless."

"It wasn't harmless to me! And why did you disregard the surfing we did on our first date when she asked?"

He blinked. "I didn't. I said 'not really', which was true given what she asked. From what I remember, I was a lot more focused on you than I was on the surfing during that date. "

"So you can't actually have fun surfing with me because I'm not good enough?"

"I had a great time and I think we could have fun doing it again."

If we ever went surfing again. "You're not bored with me?"

He looked up and shook his head. He was getting frustrated. "What have I done that makes you think I could possibly be bored with you?"

I started to tear up. I said something that had been in the back of my mind for a while. "You can't surf or do a lot of the other thrill-seeking stuff you love so much when you're with me."

"Kristen, I'm a big boy. If I didn't think we were compatible, or if I was getting bored, or anything like that, I would just tell you. The fact is I don't feel that way. Compatibility is much more complex than shared hobbies. And a relationship is much deeper than thrilling moments. We haven't been together long, but you and I both know we have great chemistry. I'm still crazy about you, and you're still the only woman I want or need."

Warmth spread from my face around my entire body. It felt good to hear those words. Even after the day before and that morning, seeing him with Ariel had shaken my confidence in how attracted Vincent was to me. If you had shown me a picture of Ariel Diamond when I was doing my initial research on Vincent, I would have said they were a perfect match. But that was before I knew him. There was more to him than he let on to the public.

"Promise?" I asked.

"Yes," he said, smiling, "I promise."

I beamed. Vincent, as if coming to a sudden realization, jumped up and went to the counter. By the time I turned around to track him, he had a camera up and snapped a picture.

"Perfect. I'd been meaning to get a good picture of you as a keepsake." He looked at his handiwork on the camera's screen. "Take a look. I think it's a great shot."

He came over and handed me the camera. He had caught me smiling wide and staring right at the camera. I was a little teary-eyed but I still looked happy. He was right, it was a perfect shot. Candid but well-framed. A professional photographer would be proud.

"I'm getting two copies. One for the cabin and one for my condo. You don't mind do you?"

I shook my head. I pondered the significance of my portrait sitting next to his cherished photos including the one with his sister. Mine would be the only one with a single person in the photo.

"I'd get one for my office desk. But I don't want to put your job in jeopardy if your employer finds out we're together."

Night fell and we curled up outside in the beach tent watching the stars, which were much more numerous than they were in New York, where you were lucky to see any. I had put on the black lingerie I brought and we had sex that night but it was more slow and intimate than the lustful frenzy the night before. My clothes weren't torched and there wasn't any chocolate involved. Vincent came once again inside me and we cuddled afterward for the remainder of the night, sharing tender kisses and small irrelevant details about our lives.

The next day was spent packing up for travel and then traveling. It had been a mostly relaxing trip, and as we landed at JFK, I wished it could have lasted just a little longer.

Chapter Eight

By the time the cab dropped me off at my apartment, it was almost eleven p.m. Exhausted, I walked in and found Riley watching *Keeping Up With The Kardashians*. She was drinking a diet coke as always and wearing yet another pink and blue sorority t-shirt and shorts combo from when she was in college.

Riley paused her show and got up off the couch. "You're back! I didn't know if you'd be home tonight. How was the trip?"

I put my stuff down on the counter and opened the fridge hoping for something to eat. Thankfully, there was some string cheese that was mine. I grabbed it. "It was good. He has a private island with a cabin that we stayed at. The entire area is gorgeous."

"A private island? Are you *fookin* kidding me?" Riley took a seat on a stool in the kitchen, where I was standing. "I'm so jealous. Look at that tan you're getting with all these trips. I need to find myself a billionaire to jet me down to the Caribbean on the regular."

I looked down at my forearms. It hadn't even occurred to me that I would be tanning, but I was getting some pretty good color. "Dating a billionaire has its perks, I have to say."

She laughed. "Things have been quiet here."

I unwrapped my string cheese and pulled off a strand to eat. "You seem to be feeling better at least," I said, chewing.

She nodded. "That I am. Better to be bored than sick. So how is Vincent, anyway? Have you two had the talk?"

"The talk?"

"You know, boyfriend/girlfriend, that kind of thing. It's getting to be about that time, right?"

Could everyone see through me this easily? How would I ever keep dating Vincent a secret when people could read me like a book? I needed to remind myself to never, ever play poker. "We did, actually."

"Oh yeah? How did it come up? Did you start it?"

I grimaced at the memory of the previous afternoon. It had ended well, but there were some bumps. "Kind of. We actually had a bit of a fight beforehand. While we were down there we ran into an ex-girlfriend of his."

My roommate's eyes widened. "On his private island?"

I shook my head. "No, we were on a bigger island nearby grabbing lunch and supplies for the cabin."

"Oh okay. That sucks. Was she hot?"

I threw my hands up. "A little sympathy would be nice!"

She shrugged. "I'm finding out how much sympathy you need. Judging by your reaction I'm guessing she was a knockout. Sorry, that sounds brutal."

I grimaced. "She's a pro surfer. She was down there modeling, actually."

Riley's eyebrows shot up. "Did she flirt with him?"

"Oh yeah. Vincent said he thought she was testing me."

It was her turn to grimace. "How did he react?"

Remembering Vincent's reaction, or lack thereof, to Ariel's flirtations brought a fresh bubble of nausea to my stomach. "He went along with it. Didn't seem to think it was a big deal."

"I can see why you had a fight. What's this surfer chick's name?"

"Ariel Diamond. And yeah, but the talk we had about it ended up being good."

While I was talking, Riley had whipped her phone out and was tapping and swiping at the screen. Her mouth made an 'O'. "Look at those abs, *Jesus*. I'm really sorry Kristen, having a girl this hot hitting on your man had to be excruciating."

I snatched her phone from her grasp. "Riley, you're really not helping!"

She tried to grab her phone back, but I pulled it away. "I'm just getting a grasp of the situation, Kris! Give me my phone back. I promise I'll stop checking this girl out."

I shook my head. "You haven't even listened to the part that was good yet."

She made one last attempt to grab her phone away, but I was too quick for her. Finally, she put her hands in her lap. "Okay, fine. So this borderline sea nymph with abs out of an anatomy textbook shows up. Then what happens?"

I snorted. She was going to be petulant about this. "Fine. here's your phone, but no more comments about how hot Ariel is, okay? Or her body."

Riley smiled and took the phone like a child receiving candy. "Thank you. So you ran into this woman and then what?"

"Well, we were in this little general store and she comes in. Everyone is staring because she's wearing a bikini." I watched my friend carefully, but she had a better poker face than mine. "She walks up to us and calls him 'Vinny' like they were lovers."

At this, Riley laughed. "'Vinny?' Do you call him that?"

"No! I don't think it fits him at all."

She shook her head, still laughing. "Me neither."

I told her about their dating history, leaving out the part about the tattoo. Riley nodded attentively. "So it sounds like they're just friends now, right? Obviously their personal connection is helpful professionally, but he's not actually into her now."

I tapped my finger on the counter, thinking whether I should spill about the tattoo. "Well, there is one weird thing. He had a tattoo of a diamond on his ribs."

I watched Riley process for a second before her mouth dropped. "Wait. Is it for her?"

I nodded. "He got it when he was twenty."

Her mouth puckered as she considered. "He's like thirty now, right? That's a long time ago."

"Thirty-one, yeah. He says there's no reason to get it removed because they're still friends. It's not like things are ugly."

"That's fair, actually. If he still loved her but couldn't be with her, it would hurt to look at that thing every time he had his shirt off. I know when I've a bad breakup I have to get rid of everything that reminds me of the guy."

I rubbed my pinky. Sometimes you can't get rid of every reminder.

"I guess you have practice," I said.

Riley smiled. "I even throw out the underwear I'm wearing when we break up."

"What?"

She half smiled. "Sorry, TMI?"

"Good lord, yes! Why on earth would you do that?"

She closed one eye, chuckling. "Do you really want to know?"

I thought about it, but shook my head. "You're right, I don't."

She continued laughing for a minute before getting a hold of herself. "Anyway, he has this tattoo. You said there was a good part."

I told her about how Vincent had assured me, as well as the picture he took. She was impressed that he would want a photo of me for his cabin and condo. Seeing how she reacted to the story made me feel better about my reaction to the situation. It had been a bit of a shock to see him around Ariel, but all in all things had ended up in a good place.

"Well that all sounds good," she said. "I'm super happy for you. How's the other part of your relationship going?"

"Which part?"

"The sex, silly."

I blushed. Riley's mind was never far from the gutter. "It's going well."

She waited, her blue eyes urging me to go on. "'It's going well?' You can't date a man that gorgeous and leave me with that. I'm watching reality television and chugging diet coke over here."

I shrugged. It wasn't something I liked to talk about, even with Riley.

"You were on his private island. If you stayed inside and did missionary before bed, I'm going to smack you."

More heat rose to my cheeks as I thought about how far from reality Riley's insinuation was. I knew she was trying to get a rise out of me. She knew being so blunt about sex would throw me off balance. "We didn't stay inside all day, I'll say that. But that's all I'll say."

Riley jutted her lip, pouting. "Can't you throw a girl a bone?"

She was doing a good job of looking pathetic, but I held strong. "Sorry. I just don't like to talk about that stuff. You know that."

She sighed, shoulders slumped. Sitting in her sorority outfit with her blonde hair in her face on a kitchen stool, she looked almost comical. "Fine." she said after a moment. "But things are going well, all in all?"

I took a deep breath of my own. "Yeah. The thing with Ariel was scary, but the scariest part was realizing how much he's beginning to mean to me."

"Sounds like you're getting serious pretty quickly."

"I guess so," I said, surprising myself with the note of sadness in my tone.

"Is he feeling the same way?"

Was he? He had told me he was crazy about me, and being in a picture in his cabin was a nice gesture, but I just had a hard time completely trusting him. He was gone so much in so many different places, and I knew the effect he had on women. On the other hand, he really hadn't given me any reason not to trust him. Maybe it was something that would just take some time.

"He did say he was crazy about me," I said. "I don't know how much more he can do to make me know how he feels."

"The island trips are also nice. Have you thought about dropping the L-word yet?"

Panic shot through my system. Had I already fallen in love with Vincent, after years of being uninterested in men? "No. That seems pretty sudden, doesn't it? It hasn't been that long."

Riley got up and grabbed a glass of water. "It is what it is," she said. She took a sip. "No need to rush it. I was just asking. Anyway, I should probably get to bed. See you tomorrow."

I wished her good night and took the seat she had been occupying moments earlier. Did I love Vincent? Things had been moving so quickly I hadn't even paused to consider my feelings. Time was passing, though. Whether I liked it or not, my relationship with Vincent couldn't stay at the same place indefinitely.

***

When Vincent and I had landed at JFK yesterday, he'd told me he had to do a quick turnaround before he traveled back down to Brazil. He would be back as soon as he could, and would be sure to let me know. Even flying by charter as he did, I couldn't understand how he could keep up his schedule. It sounded exhausting spending so much time in so many different places.

Monday morning found me in a very familiar place: in front of my work computer. Though the office was something I was still getting used to. I spent the morning sorting my inbox and reading through the long list of office memos waiting there. While I wanted to get to work on the more interesting task of creating Vincent's investment plan, if I didn't get through these emails now they would just build up and become unmanageable. It was an important part of my job to make sure I didn't miss any communications that could be vital.

My diligence paid off when I saw an email from Carl sent ten minutes before I arrived in the office. The message said to meet him in his office at ten. He had an interesting opportunity on a potential client that he wanted to discuss. I set an alert on my calendar for the meeting and hurried through the rest of my messages.

The meeting was upon me before I could get started on the work for Vincent. I grabbed a notepad and hurried across the floor to Carl's office. This time, his door was open, though he was on the phone.

He waved me in, and I stepped inside, waiting just in front of the door. "Ted, I've got a meeting. We're going to have to continue this at lunch. Yep, got it, 12:30. Usual spot. See you then."

He hung up and turned to me. "Kristen, thanks for dropping by. Shut the door and take a seat."

I did so. Carl shuffled through some papers until he found the file he wanted. While he wasn't a luddite, he had more of a preference for dealing in paper than most of the people at the firm. It was why I was taking notes on a notepad rather than my laptop. Paying attention to little details like that was important at Waterbridge-Howser.

He clapped his hands together and rubbed them together, staring me over his glasses. "First off:

Sorenson. I haven't heard anything bad, which from my perspective means things are good. Am I right?"

I nodded. "Things are going great. Lining up the last bits of the strategy and I'll be ready to present soon."

"Great. That's a tough client, so stay on your toes, but so far it sounds like you're doing the business. Good work."

"Thank you." I smiled. Carl understood that part of being a good boss was making sure people felt appreciated when they were doing their job well. Every little bit helped.

"You deserve it. As always, let me know if I can do anything. Anyway, I brought you here because I have an interesting prospect I think you would be perfect for. Do you think you can fit another pitch into your schedule?"

Working on another new client pitch would mean many days of very long hours on top of what I was already doing for Vincent. However, as the pitch with Vincent had shown, working on new business was the best way to get bonuses and promotions. I had just received a promotion, so this probably wouldn't mean another one, but it would be another drop in the bucket for my next move. With Vincent gone as much as he was, it wasn't like I had anything pressing going on in my personal life. As I thought about it, the distraction would be welcome.

"Of course," I answered.

"Great. You're going to have an analyst working with you on this one, which should ease the burden timewise a bit. The prospect is a woman who has leveraged her fame as a fitness model by selling home fitness equipment."

Did he say fitness model? My chest tightened. However unlikely it was, I had to be sure. "Is the prospect Ariel Diamond?"

Carl frowned and looked at the file. "No. Her name is Selena Richards. Who is Ariel Diamond?"

Relief swept through my body from my chest outwards. I thought of a suitable lie to tell about Ariel. "A professional surfer I learned about while doing research for the Sorenson account," I said. That was mostly true, depending on your definition of research. "She does some fitness modeling too. Sorry for interrupting."

"You do have a good grasp of that account." He chuckled. "I have to say, it's impressive. You're really on top of that guy."

I blushed, but he was looking back at the file and didn't notice. After he had finished giving me the details about Selena Richards, he left me with instructions to get a plan of action and some materials to him by the beginning of the next week. I walked out of his office excited at the chance of another sizable client.

After I got back to my office, I texted Vincent about the news. A few hours later, he replied.

Sounds great. Will have to tell me more when we talk next. I will try to call this week.

Disappointed I wouldn't be able to talk to him that night, I texted back.

You can't get away tonight even for a little bit?

It took another fifteen minutes for him to respond.

I'll be lucky to sleep tonight, sorry. As soon as I have free time, I'll call.

Frustrated, I put the phone on my desk and went back to my work. It wasn't like I didn't have plenty to do myself. Vincent had said from the outset that he was a very busy man who usually didn't have much time to give for a real relationship. I had brushed it off then, but maybe that was a deal breaker for me. Being in a relationship with a man who was constantly continent-hopping meant spending a lot of time being basically single. That hadn't been a problem before, but now I realized I might be getting attached.

The rest of the work day passed in a blur, then the rest of the work week. The weekend passed without a call from Vincent. Whenever I texted, it would take him so long to text back that a conversation was hopeless. Another work week went by until it was Friday again. I had stayed late on Thursday working on the Richards pitch, so when my phone buzzed half an hour early on Friday morning I was upset. I picked it up and saw it was Vincent.

Happy to finally hear from him, I picked it up and answered. "Hello," I said.

"Hello, beautiful. Sorry to call so early. This is the first time I've had any free time at all in a couple weeks." He sounded exhausted.

I rubbed my eyes, trying to wake up. "I was beginning to think you'd forgotten about me. Is everything okay?"

"Just about. I'm in Lisbon right now, actually. Flew in a few hours ago. I don't know if I mentioned I was coming here."

It was a little disappointing that he hadn't told me he was traveling, but I guessed it didn't matter. As I sat up in bed, I realized I was feeling a little nauseous. "You didn't. What are you doing there?"

"More meetings. We're making a push in the European market with some of our surf swimwear."

"Sounds like life's been pretty crazy."

He sighed. "This is fairly normal to be honest. Like I told you, I'm all over the place pretty often."

My nausea was getting worse. Had the Chinese food I'd eaten for dinner the night before been bad? Maybe I just missed Vincent that much. I hoped I wasn't getting sick. Working on a pitch while you were ill was a good recipe for misery. "When do you think you'll be back?"

I heard another man's voice on Vincent's end. He cursed. "I'm sorry Kristen, I have to go. The materials for my next meeting aren't ready, apparently. I'll let you know when I'm back in New York when I have a better idea. It's going to depend on how the meetings here go. Sorry again. I'll be in touch soon."

My heart sank. Vincent's schedule was really putting a strain on our relationship. I had taken the amount I was seeing him before for granted, and even that hadn't been much. "Okay. Bye."

He hung up. I looked down at my phone and saw I still had another forty minutes before I had to get up. As I shifted to plunge back into my pillow, I felt a fresh wave of nausea. Fearing I was going to vomit, I got up and sprinted to my bathroom. I barely made it.

After that, I did feel better. I went and grabbed some soda and drank it slowly in the kitchen. The nausea seemed to have gone away almost entirely, so I decided I'd still go to work. What to do about Vincent was another story. It wasn't really his fault he was so busy, but I still felt more than a little neglected. Even though I wasn't sure exactly what else he could do, I needed to talk to him about it.

If we were going to be a couple, we wouldn't be able to keep it secret forever. Vincent *had* correctly said that having relations with clients wasn't expressly forbidden. I didn't want to broadcast our relationship to the whole office, but we could risk a nice dinner in the city. It would show how much I cared about him. Whenever Vincent did return, I resolved to invite him out for a good steak. My treat.

He ended up calling a couple days later. Apparently the response in Lisbon had been mediocre. It wasn't the end of the line for the venture, but he would be returning to New York for a few days to work with another team on how to proceed. When I told him I wanted to take him out, he sounded genuinely excited. He would be getting in late Friday morning, and we were going out Friday night, despite my protests about jet lag.

Finally, Friday evening came. Despite my busy schedule, I had managed to make time to buy a new dress for the occasion. It was a ruched sheath in black, cut slim to hang against my hips. With black stilettos, red lips, and my hair curling just right, I felt as sexy as I ever had going into a date. When I stepped out into the kitchen to show off to Riley, her jaw dropped.

"Look at you, sexy girl! I bet his mouth will be absolutely watering."

I beamed. "Thanks. Are you going out?"

She nodded. She was wearing a very short, shiny blue dress that made me guess she was clubbing. "Yeah, me and the girls are going prowling tonight. I'm actually going out to grab some early drinks at Jen's before we get dinner and go dancing. Who knows, maybe I'll snag my own billionaire. Where are you two headed?"

"Strip House. After all these Caribbean weekends I figure I can treat him to a nice steak."

Our door buzzer went off. I looked at the oven clock: seven on the dot. Harried as he probably was from traveling, he was right on time. After saying a quick goodbye to Riley and grabbing my clutch, I hurried down to meet Vincent outside.

He was leaning against a streetlight post, looking at his watch like he was posing for a picture. He wore a black button down with the sleeves rolled up and black pants. His skin had the golden color of a man who had been spending a lot of time in a tropical climate. Our days apart had already caused me to forget just how attractive I found him. The way he stood there, I had half a mind to invite him up to my apartment so I could get my hands on him immediately.

He looked up and straightened. I watched him take in my appearance for the evening. Moving his eyes from my legs up to my eyes, he smiled. "Hello, Kristen."

I beamed. "Hello, Vincent."

"I like the outfit." He stepped toward me and bent down to whisper in my ear. "It'll look even better pooled on the floor."

I pressed my cheek into his chest. "I think you're right. But we need to get ourselves fed first."

He took my hand. "Where to?"

"I made reservations at Strip House. It's nice out, so I think we should just walk."

Vincent looked around, then shrugged. "Lead the way."

We made it to Strip House twenty minutes later, holding hands the whole way. The restaurant was decorated in an 1890s bordello style, with red wallpaper and low lighting. The Zagat Guide had been right: this definitely felt romantic and even a little naughty. I was very pleased with the selection.

Vincent looked around and took everything in. "Nice choice," he said. As the hostess took us to our seat, he slid his hand down my back, fingering the band of my underwear through my dress.

I shuddered at the intimate gesture. Thoughts of how the evening might end sent a surge of heat through my body. Every touch he gave me merely made me want him even more. The way I craved him bordered on scary: I had been working for the past two years to be a very self-sufficient person, but there was no replacement for his hands on my body.

We took our seats and ordered quickly. I got a bottle of malbec to split between the two of us, and we both ordered steak. Vincent looked more relaxed than I had thought he would. Yet again, I was impressed with his ability to switch between modes seamlessly.

We made chit-chat until the wine came. I had decided I wanted to wait until I had a little liquid courage before I brought up the topic of his schedule. There was still no answer popping out at me as far as what he could do, but I thought having the fact that it was bothering me on his radar wouldn't hurt. If he got offended about it, then maybe, as much as it hurt, having him out of my life would be for the best. Some kind of balance between work and life was important to me in whoever I ended up with. As crazy as it sounded to me, I realized that thinking about him in those terms wasn't too far-fetched. Of course, that was just my perspective. I wasn't sure if he felt the same way.

Once the wine came, I took a big sip. When I looked at Vincent, I could tell he was watching me carefully. He knew me well enough to know something was up.

"So," I said, gathering myself, "how was your trip?"

He scrunched his eyebrows. "Fine. Business. Is there something you want to say?"

I took a deep breath. "You were gone a long time."

"I know. It was exhausting."

"Is that normal for you?"

He chewed his lip. "Yes and no. It happens. When you run a business, sometimes you just have to be the person to handle things."

"Can't you just delegate to someone else and fire them if they do it poorly?"

A fire broke out behind his eyes as he continued to work his jaw. "I could, sure. I could do whatever I wanted."

The intensity with which he had begun to speak startled me. I knew I could guess the answer to the following question, but I asked anyway. "So why don't you?"

"Because there are a lot of people whose jobs depend on my company being good at what it does, and I owe it to all of them to make my company the best I can make it."

I found myself nodding before I realized it. It was a more altruistic answer than I was expecting.

"Besides," he continued, "I'm thirty one. Not exactly pushing retirement age. As successful as I've been, I still have ambitions to push the company further."

That was closer to the answer I had guessed. "Where do I fit into these plans?" I asked. Tears fought to come out, but I held them back. I didn't want to be crying for this conversation, especially in public.

His expression softened. "I'm still figuring that out. Believe me, it's not absent from my mind."

"These past two weeks were very hard for me. I felt like I was just another thing on your todo list."

He sighed. "Kristen, I told you at the Knicks game that I'm a very busy man."

"I know. And I brushed it off at the time. But it's becoming a problem for me." I was still holding on without crying, but I didn't know how much more of this conversation I could take before the waterworks started.

It was strange not being able to control my emotions better in public.

He took another deep breath. His thin lips and squinting eyes signaled to me he was thinking hard about what he was going to say next. I waited. Finally, he spoke. "I just need some time to figure out how to make it work. You're important to me. I think I've shown you that so far. Even if I'm not perfect, I want to make this work, and I tend to get what I want when I put my mind to it." He smiled. "Just please be patient. I'm working on it."

It was as good an answer as I could expect. A smile crept over my faith. I was relieved that he hadn't gotten too defensive. He was right: we hadn't been dating that long. I couldn't expect him to change his lifestyle overnight. If he was working on it, that was enough.

I heard his phone buzz. He reached into his pocket and checked his phone quickly before looking up at me. "Sorry, that's set to only vibrate when it's from an important number. But tonight's just between us. It can wait. I'm leaving this here while I go to the men's room so you don't think I'm sneaking away for business, okay?"

I was surprised at the way his brown eyes searched my face. His expression showed how seriously he was taking our conversation. I nodded my assent. "Thank you for listening to me," I said. "It means a lot."

I could see him relax as he smiled. "I'm trying. Be right back."

Sure enough, he left the phone next to his silverware. I watched it, musing on how many people must be trying to reach Vincent at all hours around the world. That he was the nexus of such a huge enterprise was amazing. Sure, I had to keep my work phone on me at all times, but that was mostly to answer to my bosses. When people went to Vincent, it was because they had decided he needed to know something. He wanted that communication.

His phone flashed—though it didn't vibrate—and despite my instincts toward respecting his privacy, I looked. What kinds of things were people sending to Vincent at all hours? I thought it would probably be something almost indecipherable to me: earnings reports, internal memos, or something similar. Instead it was a text message. I read the name upside down and felt my throat tighten up.

The text was from Ariel Diamond. I reached across the table and snatched up his phone to read the message properly.

Hey Vinny! Had so much fun riding your COCK ;-)

My stomach dropped. My mouth tasted like acid. I wanted to throw the phone across the room. The wine along with it. The room felt as though it were turning like Vincent's speed boat. I felt so sick I thought I might vomit in the restaurant.

He fucked Ariel Diamond while he was on his 'business' trip.

Mixing business with pleasure. I was almost more angry at myself for being such a fool than at him. How could I have fallen for his stupid charming words?

I inhaled a shaky breath and got up from the table. Vincent could get this bill without a problem. In fact, he should. I wanted nothing to do with him.

Tears flooded my vision as I left the restaurant.

I was too shocked to feel anything but numbness. How could he do that to me? After he had reassured me so convincingly that he didn't have feelings for Ariel anymore, he had sex with her. Just like that. It probably didn't even mean anything to him. Maybe he didn't have feelings for her and just had sex with her because he thought he could get away with it and needed a stress reliever. What were the chances I would find out, after all? I was all the way back in New York, trusting that he wasn't calling because he was too busy. With work, of course.

I found a cab and got in. Minutes later I was at my apartment. I gave the driver a twenty dollar bill and didn't wait for the change. Vision still blurry with tears, I unlocked my apartment door and stepped inside. The place was empty; Riley must've already left with her girlfriends. I briefly entertained the idea of joining them but thought better of it. Being around people wasn't what I needed right now. For now, I just wanted to be alone in my bed to cry.

My phone had been vibrating in my purse the whole cab ride home. I didn't dare look at it. Vincent surely had some brilliant excuse for that message, but I didn't even want to hear his voice right now. As I replayed our relationship in my head, I couldn't believe how foolish I had been. Of course a risk-taking billionaire like him wouldn't want to be locked down with someone like me. I was too safe, too boring to satisfy his needs. Sure, sometimes he wanted someone safe to come home to, but that would never be enough.

He would always want more.

My phone buzzed again. Annoyed, I pulled it out of my clutch. Sure, enough, it was Vincent. He had called ten times and sent two text messages. I didn't read them before I hit the phone's power button. Maybe I never would. I could have Riley turn on my phone and delete them for me.

A fresh wave of nausea and tears overtook me. I lay down on my bed and cried as hard as I ever had. Each sob shook my body so hard it was painful. At times it was hard to catch my breath, but still it kept coming. I just couldn't believe he had done that. How could he? Right when I had finally opened myself up, he had stabbed me square in the back and twisted the knife for good measure.

Dimly I heard a pounding at the door. He'd followed me home. I sat up and looked at the makeup smudging my pillow. Great, another piece of laundry.

I probably looked like a raccoon. Even so, I couldn't have him pounding on that door forever. My neighbors would file a noise complaint against me. I went to the door.

"Go away," I yelled. "I can't even look at you right now."

The pounding stopped for a second, then became a knock. I was surprised he hadn't yelled back. Typical Vincent, to have a measured response at a time like this. Where previously I had admired the way he could control himself, now I was thinking he might be some kind of robot.

Maybe he would go away if I just screamed at him to his face. I opened the door, and was greeted by a man that wasn't Vincent.

My head felt like a helium balloon. The blue eyes behind the man's rimless glasses sparked with an angry intensity I'd thought I'd left behind.

It was Marty.

Thank you for reading!

If you could spare a moment to leave a
review it would be much appreciated.

Reviews help new readers find my books and
decide if it's right for them. It also provides
valuable feedback for my writing!

Sign up for my mailing list to find out when the next book the Surrender Series is released!
http://eepurl.com/sH7wn

0418

Made in the USA
Lexington, KY
14 May 2014